FIRST STRIKE

FIRST STRIKE

CHRISTOPHER VERSPEAK

mantic

Mantic Entertainment LTD.

193 Hempshill Lane, Bulwell, Nottingham, NG6 8PF

ISBN: 978-1-911516-00-2

Copyright © 2016 by Mantic Games.

Find out more about Mantic Games at
www.manticgames.com

First published 2016

Editing: Stewart Gibbs

Design and Layout: Karen Miksza

Cover Art: Eric Wilkerson

Printing and Binding:
Aurumprint, Vilnius, Lithuania Sv. Stepono g. 27c-5, LT-01315

"The best weapon against an enemy is another enemy."

- Friedrich Nietzsche

CHAPTER 1

Guiders City, the garden city built at the edge of the desert, had finally burned. It had been a long time coming, some of the old timers said. Others said it had come none too soon.

Fires had burned in the low-rises and the culture sinks, the office blocks and the municipal kiosks alike. The flames had burnt out most of the illicit caff joints and flop-shops around the west side of the Senega Memorial Spaceport, the ones used by the off-duty shippers and couriers between runs to sleep off their fatigue or the narcs they had consumed. They had shattered the glass of the legal and licensed fashion joints and eateries on the east side too. The fires did not care what they destroyed.

They had left their mark long after they had been extinguished. Every building, street, and structure that had not been burned to the ground was coated in the dust and ash left by those that had.

The city had been built on a peninsula, with desert plains to the north and sea on every other side. Sand blown down from the deserts had begun to pile up on the streets,

7

forming long pale drifts at the base of the remaining buildings, including the vertical farms.

Stretching nearly a kilometre into the sky, each farm consisted of a dozen or so massive discs, piled one atop another like stacks of coins radiating from a central column. The columns contained numerous powerful motors that could rotate the discs around the axis in response to the data collected by barometric analysers and thermometers. They were designed to optimise the sunshine each hectare of land received and protect them from any harsh winds. Many still did, as they were powered by solar collectors and so were entirely independent of the city's shredded electrical grid. They still relied on fresh water from the city's desalination plant though, and that had been cut off too.

As the sun of the Acreon system began to set beneath the horizon to the city's west, tower G3's motor systems activated and several of the farm's lower layers began to rotate, chasing the fading light in a slow clockwise motion. G3's on-board computer had calculated this to be a necessary step to maximise the output of the levels involved. But, as mathematically capable as it was, the computer was completely unaware its movement was futile. The soil on its discs was all parched and barren, cracked brown dirt dredged from the depths of Acreon's oceans, completely dry for the first time in aeons.

Without a supply of fresh water the farms in Guiders could no longer produce the crops of caffa beans it had been hoped would fund the colony's continued existence. Nor could any food fit for human consumption be grown and so most of Guiders' residents had quit the city. Some had gone to other, smaller colonies further inland. Many more had fled to the safety of other worlds entirely, because starvation was not the only danger in Guiders City.

The city had not been entirely deserted though. As the upper levels of G3 slid into place with a heavy clunk, near the base of its giant tower a squad of soldiers paused in their patrol of the otherwise silent streets.

They had gathered around the entrance to a low build-ing set between two of the farms. The faded plastic sign attached to its roof bore the remains of a company logo, marking it out as an official admin building. But it was the broken glass of its doors, locked tight as they were, that interested the soldiers.

The marines worked in pairs, most of them setting up in covering positions along the street nearby, simultaneously setting up overwatch and finding shelter from the still-warm sun, but three of them kneeled near the building's doors. One of the trio quickly unhitched the bulky pack she had carried through the heat of Guiders' streets and set it down on the sandy ground.

She pulled out an extendable wand from one corner of the pack and pulled the canvas cover partway off the box within it. Then she extended the wand through a crack in the panel at the base of the door and waited for the box to do its work. The unit's sergeant and lieutenant crouched down beside her, their rifles cradled loosely across their knees.

"Ok, Niles, tell me what we've got."

"Roger that, Sergeant Thole." said the kneeling marine, trying to imitate enthusiasm. She, like most of the marines in the platoon, was of the opinion that today's detail was a waste of time, just as it had been on the previous three days they had been assigned it. But Niles knew it did not pay to aggravate an officer, no matter what your opinion was of them or of the duty they had volunteered you for.

It took the sensor box a few seconds to do its job, sampling the air a few hundred times and running it through a spectrographic analyser. It was a rough process, but effective. The box beeped disconsolately, as it had every other time the unit had stopped to investigate a building with a broken door or smashed window that day. It could find no pheromonal indicator of Veer-myn within the building and Niles wasted no time in withdrawing the sensor from the other side of the door. She looked up at Thole with an 'I told you so' look on her face and began to pack the detector away.

"Hey, that's another ten you owe me, Stiller."

Corporal Stromer had taken a position kneeling down beside the broken remains of a duracrete planter. Its soil had spilled out onto the pavement beside it through a massive crack in its side and what was left of the plants within it was an unidentifiable dry brown. He stood up as he watched Niles heft the pack back onto her shoulders and smiled as he walked towards another of the marines who taken cover behind a burned out delivery truck a few metres away.

Stiller sighed as he stood up too. "Add it to my tab."

"Well, someone's got to get something out of us being out here." Stromer said, still smiling. In truth though, he was as tired as they all were of the endless patrols the squad had been volunteered for.

Their company, Drakenhof Marine, had been contracted to Acreon some weeks previously. Their mission brief, as explained by the commandant of the expeditionary force assigned to Acreon at their training depot on Karkorum, had been that the company was deploying to put down a Veer-myn uprising.

There was some novelty about the assignment – normally the Veer-myn that lived across the GCPS were not considered dangerous enough to warrant the use of as prestigious a company as theirs. But the Veer-myn on Acreon had done something unusual too.

Instead of stealthily infiltrating, as Veer-myn were generally known to do, they had arrived using some sort of as-yet unidentified aerial assault mechanism. Their attack had caused widespread damage to corporate property and personnel and had also disturbed the Veer-myn already living on Acreon. This first nest was hidden somewhere beneath Guiders City but the resultant internecine conflict had spilled out above ground. The Veer-myn had created enough turmoil that someone had made the call to Drakenhof Marine to eliminate the alien threat completely.

The expeditionary force had shipped out almost immediately – fast deployment was one of the hallmarks and major selling points of a Drakenhof force – with nearly two hundred frontline troops and half as many again in support staff. But the men and women of Falcon squad had ended up late to the party.

They had been forced to delay their transit from Karkorum, missing the departure of the expedition's assigned assault cruiser, the MSS Genoa, while they waited for their new officer, Lt. Pieter Ammit, to arrive from an officer training program on the Drakenhof homeworld's second moon. It had been an inauspicious start to the campaign and not one that had set relations between the men and their new commander on the best footing.

By the time they had secured passage aboard one of the

few merchant vessels going towards the Euxine sector and finally arrived at Sword Base, the camp the expeditionary force on Acreon had built around Guiders City's eastern shuttleport, it seemed the best of the fighting had already been done. Other units had been battling in the streets of Guiders for nearly a G-standard month when Falcon finally made it to the planet's surface and they were more than happy to regale the latecomers with tales of combat and glory. The streets, they said, had been alive with Veer-myn – the place had virtually been a shooting gallery. But now most of them were dead. This did not sit well with any of the marines, something their new lieutenant was well aware of.

The operation had moved into its next phase. A dragnet approach had been drawn up, with patrols being sent out on a constant basis to clear the outlying areas of the city, using bio-sniffers to track down any small gangs of Veer-myn and locate any stranded human survivors. The cordon would be tightened with every patrol, forcing what Veer-myn were left towards the centre of the city and, hopefully, locating the entrance to their nest along the way. Several tankers filled with incendiary gel had been shipped in especially for this final phase of the op.

Lt. Ammit had made it his personal mission to see that the squad took as many patrol missions as they could, but whether his primary motivation was to help his men see combat before it was all over or to help his superiors see him being an effective leader was a matter of much debate amongst the platoon. Whatever his reasons, three solid days of marching through Guiders' dry and dusty streets under a bright hot sun, checking every crack and crevice in the city, was wearing them all down.

Ammit pulled out a digital reader from a pouch on his webbing. It contained location tracking software and a map of the city. He tried to remain professional, despite the disappointment he too felt at once more not finding an enemy to fight.

"Ok, people," he said, "That's another one down. Rains, mark it up. I'm going to call Sword, get our next target.

The others murmured their assent and Rains, the newest member of the unit, pulled a can of spray paint from a pocket on his fatigues. He walked over to the glass doors and began to mark them out with the squad's numeric designation and then the letters 'C' and 'E' to denote that they had checked the building and found it empty.

Rains had been handed this duty by the unanimous vote of the rest of the squad, having only joined them a few weeks before the lieutenant. He was, to most of them, 'the rookie', or 'the rook' and whenever there was an unpleasant duty to be done, Rains got it.

He had expected a degree of hazing from his new unit when he came to Drakenhof. It was a rite of passage for anyone joining such a tightly-knit group and something he had known he would have to put up with. But he was a Core-worlder too, born and raised there, and he knew that was a source of resentment for some of the older members of the unit too.

The Galactic Co-Prosperity Sphere, or GCPS as it was commonly known, had grown, from a relatively modest collection of worlds now known as the Core, through a series of expansionary pushes, or 'Spheres', into one of the largest and wealthiest known territories in the galaxy. Each new Sphere had brought dozens of new star systems within the administrative borders of the GCPS and added the wealth of countless potential sources of exploitable assets to the GCPS's balance sheets.

In theory, the free markets and movement of goods and people across the galaxy benefited them all, and the power and wealth of the GCPS as a whole was undisputed. But there was still a fairly common feeling amongst its citizens, one that grew stronger the closer one got to the edge of GCPS space, that its power was often-as-not used to funnel the wealth towards the Core.

"You're still too shiny." was what Beggs, the rookie's fire-team partner had told Rains in his usual thin, reedy whisper that morning. They were gearing up for the day's patrol in their barracks and Rains' first instinct had been to check his armour.

"I'm too what?" Rains had asked.

"No, not your gear. You." Beggs had stated. "You've still got that Core shine on you. That First Sphere polish. And no one out here likes that shine."

Rains had tried not to be offended as his Beggs walked slowly away from him.

Beggs himself was perhaps as far from being a shiny Core-worlder as was possible. He would claim, if questioned, that his voice had been made hoarse by years of working in a vapour mine on the Orion Shoulder, a job he had taken to get out of a bar debt he ran up in a Grogan joint before he knew better. Most of the time, this explanation would be accepted. But Beggs carried a long scar that ran across his throat, almost from ear to ear. Most of the time it could pass without notice – it was pale and thin, as if at least some measure of regenics had been applied in order to blend it into the surrounding skin. But sometimes, particularly when Beggs had thrown back one too many shots in whatever bar he had fallen into and the rest of his face had gone red with the effort of singing bawdy songs, the evidence of a cut was more obvious.

The justice system of Orion's Shoulder was notorious throughout most of the GCPS – a rough and ready 'frontier' style of crime and punishment that had persisted even after the sector was folded into the Third Sphere. However, there were still only a few crimes likely to be deemed sufficiently heinous to warrant the kind of retribution that would give a man a scar like Beggs wore under his chin. The rumour was, his criminal record was such that finding regular employment was no longer possible, that for Beggs Drakenhof was the only option.

No one ever raised the issue with him – no one sober anyway – and it certainly did not matter to the company. The Drakenhof clan were connected enough and powerful enough and, most importantly, rich enough, that once you were in their employ, there were very few individuals in the entire galaxy who could pull you back out again. If you carried out the terms of your contract faithfully the Drakenhofs would protect you. To them, there was really no better qualification for a term of service as a corporate marine than a record of violence.

His job done, Rains joined Beggs and the rest of the squad where they had gathered in the lee of a burnt-out qwik-food kiosk, out of earshot of their sergeant and lieutenant. They could still hear Ammit though, as he tried to make contact with Drakenhof base.

"You think he can get that thing working?" Stromer asked. Ammit was working a handheld microphone that was connected to a radio transceiver fitted onto his armour. A few of the marines had them but their effectiveness had been patchy at best.

One of the other marines looked up at the sky and sniffed.

"I doubt it," he said. "There's a storm coming."

"How can you tell?" Rains asked. The sky seemed a cloudless blue to him.

Stromer laughed quietly.

"Son, King here is a genuine native, born and bred." he said.

"That true, Corporal?" Rains said.

King nodded slowly.

"Yeah. It's true."

Even though the sun was setting, the heat at street level was still punishingly hot. A swirl of wind blew warm gritty dust up in their faces as they walked. Stromer pulled the end of the flexible tube attached to his drinking bladder from the webbing on his shoulder and took a long drag.

"So tell us, local boy," he said. "Why in the Core would the Veer-myn would want to come here?"

Like Stromer, King wore a corporal's stripe, but instead of a rifle he carried the platoon's heavy support weapon, a drum-fed BG-03M grenade launcher, on a sling over his shoulder. He too took a swig from his own hydration pack, swishing the water over his dry gums before swallowing. He shook his head slowly.

"You got me." he said. "I couldn't wait to get away."

"Doesn't look like there's much here but dust and dirt." Rains said.

King nodded. "Yeah, that's what I thought too."

He was the home-town boy, but he didn't feel much like verbally defending Acreon. For that matter, he wasn't entirely sure why he and his unit were being asked to fight for it either.

Acreon, or EX567/4 as it was coded in official records, was

a Fourth Sphere world, one of several small planets located in the Euxine sector almost at the very north-western edge of the GCPS. It was currently designated in those same records as a desert planet, despite much of its surface being covered by water. This was because its seas were hyper-salinated and unfit for natural human consumption or usage – something that had not been adequately understood before nearly fifty thousand eager colonists, including King's parents, had arrived there on one-way transport barges.

The planet was almost unbearably hot most of the time and fresh water was in scarce supply. Much of the continent the first settlers found themselves deposited on was covered by desert terrain, vast tracts of sand and wilderness.

But there were a few places less hostile to life than the rest of the planet and the founders of the new colony had taken on the challenge. They had employed experimental tech, like that found in the tower farms but at a smaller scale, to turn the saline water of the seas into potable liquid. Then they turned the algae that grew out on those same waters into food, and finally, in time, built the new lives they had been looking for.

Guiders City had been built at the tip of a narrow peninsula jutting out into Acreon's seas. It was the first large settlement on Acreon and was still the largest population centre on the planet. It had weathered many storms since its founding, both literal and metaphorical, as it struggled to make its place in the ever-expanding GCPS.

"Leave him alone, rook," said Stromer. "Core knows I wouldn't be here either if I had any choice."

"Doesn't matter why they came." Stiller was King's fire-team partner and he raised his weapon as if aiming it at an unseen enemy in the middle of the road and mimed the weapon recoiling as he fired it. "They're all going straight to hell when we find them."

There were a few approving murmurs from the rest of the unit, but King could tell there wasn't a lot of conviction behind them. It was beginning to feel like there weren't any more Veer-myn left to find. The Veer-myn had made their presence known on Acreon in an uncharacteristically explosive way, but now they had seemed to melt away into the shadows.

"Ok, people, we got a target!"

Their discussion was interrupted as Ammit pulled out a map-reader from a pouch on his waist and began plotting a route with the squad's sergeant.

"Well I'll be damned," said Stiller. "Lieutenant Too-Late got us something to kill."

Stromer shrugged noncommittally.

"We'll see." he said.

"Alright, people, break-time's over. It's time to get paid!" Sergeant Thole was marching towards them, a bright look in his eyes.

"King, you and Stiller got point." he said. "Head east, standard dispersal. Let's move it people – there's things waiting to get killed out there!"

CHAPTER 2

The squad moved out, heading towards the target the commanders at Sword Base, Drakenhof Marine's camp on Acreon had identified. They moved quickly but professionally, the pairs of marines covering each other as they advanced along the dusty road. King and Stiller led the way.

So much of the place was familiar to King – the dun coloured buildings, the smell of the desert nearby and of the sea. The feeling of building electricity in the air that had told him a sandstorm was building out amongst the dunes. Only the sound of the wind whistling between the layered farmland was new. Construction on the first tower was only nearing completion when he had boarded the shuttle that had taken him off-world as a young man. Now there were a dozen of them.

They were coming to the end of the line of farm towers and nearing the edge of a more built-up district. Beneath the gaudy advertising hoardings on the structures ahead of them, King could see the outlines of Shensig tiles. He knew that signalled the beginning of the warren of narrow streets and buildings dating back to the colony's foundation.

Ammit called a halt as they approached a junction where the road branched off to the left and right. At the centre of the junction was a large warehouse retail outlet. A dust-caked red and white plastic logo bolted onto the front of the building's wide roof proclaimed it was a Buy-M-All, the kind of place that in better days in Guiders would have sold everything from spare parts for the farms to recliner couches for the farmers' homes. It was likely one of the last places in the city that still had stocks of food too.

There was a wrecked municipal waste vehicle sitting burnt-out by the side of the road and the squad moved into cover behind it.

"Oneyul," Thole said, "You're up."

Two marines moved up the line to join the sergeant and Ammit as they scanned the storefront.

Oneyul was the unit's best shot, holding several divisional records for marksmanship. Rumour had it she had once shot a Marauder commander through his bionic eye from a distance of no less than five hundred metres. Her company-issued weapon was fitted with an expensive Accutek scope she had purchased herself and it was trained on the doors off the Buy-M-All in front of her.

Her fire-team partner, Vallow, was not a bad shot himself – he had once had a try-out as a Jack for no less a team than the Trontek 29ers. But injury had ended his playing career, and pushed him towards private military work. Now he guarded his team-mate's flank with his rifle.

"What can you see, Private?" Ammit said. He had his own field optic out and was looking through it, holding the monocular up to one eye.

Oneyul didn't move, keeping her weapon trained on the Buy-M-All doors as she spoke quietly.

"Nothing on my scope she said. There're too many obstructions," she said quietly. "Thought I heard something though…"

Behind her, King tried to follow the sharpshooter's sightline. The front of the warehouse store was largely glass, but what wasn't covered with a pale grey layer of dirt and dust was obscured by promotional posters advertising the latest goods being offered by the store. There were two sets of double-doors leading inside, the kind that would automatically open when their sensors detected approaching customers, and the one on the right-hand side of the building was sealed tightly shut. The set on the left though was slightly ajar, with a gap between the two doors that looked like it might be just wide enough for a small human, or a Veer-myn, to fit through.

"I can't hear anything." Stromer whispered behind him.

King couldn't either. The wind was howling through the upper levels of the towers behind them now as the storm he had predicted moved in.

"Are we sure this is it?" Stromer said.

At the head of the line, Ammit had replaced his optic and was hastily checking his map-reader.

"This is the place," he said. "I'm sure of it."

He looked back up at the store.

"I can't see any movement either though." said Ammit. "Sergeant?"

Thole was scanning the front of the suspicious building with his rifle's built-in scope. After a moment he shook his head too.

But then they all heard it – the faint sound of smashing glass from within the outlet. Then came the sound of something heavy being dragged and then more breaking glass.

21

"Looters?" Rains whispered from the back of the line.

"Could be." Stromer said. "Wanna go in and find out?"

"I don't think so." whispered King. "The locals know we're out here, they know better than to get in the way.

Ammit slid his reader back into its pouch.

"Well, somebody's in there. What do you think, Sergeant?" he said.

Thole hesitated. He was older than the new officer, older than most of the marines in his platoon in fact, and had years of experience to draw on. He considered the wide, low facade of the building facing his unit.

"Sir, we don't know what or who is in there." he said in a low voice. "Could be looters, could be 'crawlers. Could just be locals who haven't evacuated yet and are looking for food."

"Agreed. What would you recommend?"

Thole looked towards the building then at the marines behind him.

"Might be worth calling it in. Or trying to, anyway. See if we can get some backup out here."

Beside King, Stiller frowned. The conversation was being relayed to each marine through relays built into their helmets and he keyed on his own mic.

"Sir, with all due respect," he said. "We do that, we lose the element of surprise."

Ammit looked at the marine, a questioning look on his face. Stiller ignored the darker expression on his sergeant's.

"Sir, the rules of engagement are pretty clear. Anything out here that's not wearing our colours is to be considered a threat. If it's looters, whether they're local or not, we're contracted to stop them. It's in the brief. They're a threat to the stability of the colony. And if it's Veer-myn – well,

22

either way we're covered. But if we just sit out here twiddling our thumbs, whoever is in there could be getting away. And then there's always the second possibility."

"Which is?" King had joined in the debate.

"That there is nobody in there – it's just actual rats. Or whatever the hell it is they have on this Core-forgotten world. No offense, King."

"None taken."

"And if that's the case, do we really want to be the team that spent three days searching for Veer-myn and then called in the cavalry when we got spooked by yet another empty building?"

King sighed. He hated to admit it, but his fire-team partner did have a point. He knew Thole was no fool either though. Moving into a large unknown building like the Buy-M-All so close to nightfall while searching for dangerous aliens was a risky proposition.

Ammit frowned and looked back towards the building in the distance as he considered his options. Finally he turned back, facing the rest of his team.

"Ok, let's see if we can flush them out." He turned towards his corporal, one eye on King's grenade launcher. "King."

"Sir?"

Ammit gestured towards the warehouse ahead.

"One round, right through the doors. Can you do that for me?"

"Sir, I –" Ammit raised a hand to silence Thole.

"King. One round, straight in. COSH canister. Can you do that?"

This time it was Stiller who protested but Ammit silenced him too with a look.

"I understand the ROE, Corporal, but I won't have us

23

firing lethal rounds until I know what we're firing at. King?"

Stiller looked away, disappointed with his commander's interpretation of the rules, but King nodded. Although he knew Stromer was technically correct – Drakenhof had been contracted to clear the city of all threats – the idea of lobbing a high-explosive charge indiscriminately into what was still a civilian building was not one he found attractive.

"Yes, sir." he said. "I can do that."

The BG-03M tactical munitions launcher was one of the most widely used specialist weapons in the GCPS. It was bulkier than a rifle, but its designers had done well to streamline the firing mechanism and munitions storage capacity of the much heavier vehicle-mounted BG-02 version into a man-portable weapon. It did not have the same range as a rifle though, and King needed to advance a few metres along the street in order to fire on the building.

He and Stiller sprinted towards an overturned municipal waste bin that lay near the entrance to Buy-M-All. The heat-spoiled refuse that had spilled out of it stank badly, but its metal sides provided ample cover and a good view of the front of the store.

The rest of the unit had fanned out behind them, setting up as much covering fire on the front of the building as they could, all of them ready to open up on anything that threatened King and Stiller or to move in and clear the building. That would be their last option though as it was potentially the most dangerous manoeuvre a lightly armoured unit like theirs could be expected to undertake. Far better to flush whoever or whatever was inside out and into the open and onto territory of their own choosing, where the marines could employ their massed firepower.

King pulled out the feeder drum from his weapon and flipped open the single-round charging port on its side. Then he pulled out a COSH canister round from the bandolier he wore across his chest and placed it into the port, locking the slide cover over it and switching back on its electronic trigger.

The high-ex rounds he would normally fire were ringed with red and marked with the skull and crossbones symbol that had symbolised violent death almost since the invention of writing, but the COSH canister was unmarked apart from a green band around its base. He carried fewer of them but they were standard issue for urban pacification ops, which technically was what Acreon was. It was filled with a non-lethal, but highly debilitating version of the gas used by riot cops across the GCPS. It would induce nausea and vomiting in most carbon-based, oxygen-breathing subjects, as well as tears and disorientation. It was not intended to have a lethal effect, but it would certainly give lifeforms caught in its cloud a strong incentive to seek fresh air and outdoor spaces as soon as possible.

He checked over his shoulder that the rest of the unit was in position and, when Ammit gave him a thumbs-up, stood and aimed his weapon over the waste bin at the Buy-M-All, lining up its laser crosshairs on the gap in the doors on the left of the building. Stiller stood beside him.

"Three, two, one."

King squeezed the trigger on the launcher and felt the weapon buck slightly as it fired, a loud percussive 'pop' noise sending the round towards its target. His aim was good but not perfect. The canister arced through the air and missed the gap in the doors by nearly a metre, instead crashing through the glass panel in the door on the left.

"Damnit," said Stiller.

King looked over at his partner. "What?"

"That's another ten I owe Stromer."

"Sorry." said King.

They heard a small bang and there was a flash of white light from within the store as the round went off. Thin fingers of yellow smoke began to stream out of the hole King had made and from the gap between the doors. But that was all. No stream of coughing, retching refugees or aliens followed them and King began to wonder if Stiller's suggestion the building might be just another empty shell had been on the money.

Then, suddenly, pandemonium broke out as five scrawny figures smashed through the doors on the right. A cloud of noxious yellow gas billowed around them but their clawed hands, double-jointed legs and long thick tails were unmistakeable – they were Veer-myn, and they were running. There was a narrow alley between the warehouse and the neighbouring building and as the sun glinted off the broken glass behind them, the Veer-myn gang sprinted into it.

"Light 'em up!" yelled Stiller.

The platoon opened fire and a flashing fusillade of bright blue energy blasts strobed into the store's walls, shattering its glass front and causing the doors the Veer-myn had escaped through to collapse groaning to the floor. The Veer-myn were too fast though and they all darted out of sight along the alley, apparently unhurt by either the COSH gas or the marines' fire.

"Did you see that?" shouted an excited Rains to the platoon, "They were wearing gas masks!"

King had opened the breach of his launcher again and was reloading the drum of lethal rounds as the rest of the platoon ran up to his position. This time there was no hesitation by the lieutenant. His team had found Veer-myn, real live legit targets, and he would not deny his men the chance to engage and destroy them.

"After them!" shouted Ammit. Almost as one the unit followed him as he ran toward the alley they had seen the Veer-myn flee into.

Stromer patted King on the shoulder as he ran past him. "Great shot, man!"

King scowled as he snapped his weapon closed and rearmed its electronic systems. The platoon was entering the oldest and densest part of the city, streets he hadn't walked for nearly a decade, but that he knew would be difficult to navigate and full of danger. Streets that would be difficult to reach even for air-cover. He wondered if he had brought enough ammunition for what lay ahead.

His weapon beeped its readiness and he stood and ran after the others.

CHAPTER 3

A lone figure watched as the marines ran into the alley, chasing after the Veer-myn gang whose looting they believed they had interrupted.

He was practically invisible. There was a low parapet around the roof and it obscured most of his form from sight. What it did not hide was covered by a crypsis cloak.

The light-bending properties of the material, draped as it was over his helmet and armoured shoulders and carefully folded around the long barrel of his customised rifle, gave his image a mirage-like quality, making him all but indistinguishable from his surroundings. The cloak was rated as being effective up to a metre away on a stationary wearer, at least for standard vision types, and he knew it was highly unlikely anyone or anything could ever get that close to him without him seeing them coming first anyway.

Seeing things coming was, after all, a large part of his job.

He had followed the marine unit at a discrete distance for some time. He had trailed other units from their company before that too. Although he had been on Acreon for some time now, he had not revealed his presence or that of his team to the marines' commanders. It was not a matter of any arrogance or pride on his part – he knew he would need to introduce himself at some point. But the nature of his mission could make that difficult.

His team had arrived on Acreon at almost the same time the marines had. Experience had taught him though that when dealing with un-enhanced humans, particularly in outer-sphere worlds, it often paid to find out who and what he was dealing with first. So he had watched the marines build their camp and begin their campaign to retake this city from the Veer-myn. He had noted their performance as much as the aliens'.

The Drakenhof soldiers seemed well-drilled and were certainly well-equipped. He had seen enough small-scale engagements to convince him that though they weren't as good as he or his companions were, they were decent soldiers – for normal humans, anyway.

He had expected no less.

Drakenhof Marine had a reputation. Like many private security consultancies, the company had its fair share of blood-soaked contracts on its books. It had been engaged to do many things some of the more liberal minds back in the Core might consider unpleasant or distasteful. But they had carried them all through to completion and done so well. They got the job done, whatever it was, and this was something he could respect. They were professionals.

The patrol he had been watching today though was still running straight into the Veer-myn trap.

The soldiers were good, but their leadership was lacking.

The ten men and women had followed the Veer-myn they had found at a headlong charge without once questioning where their enemy was going. Why they were in the store or

30

why they had not fired a single shot before they fled. Now the marines were apparently completely failing to notice the way their targets were managing to always stay just out of weapons range while remaining just in visual range.

He stood and shrugged off his cloak and the mirage of his crypsis cloak dropped away. Beneath it were the much harder lines of a human male in an almost completely enclosed suit of grey and black armour. He was a stark figure, tall and imposing, standing alone on a windswept rooftop in Acreon's largest city.

Every line on his armour ran straight and every angle was sharp and severe, from the heavy pauldrons on each shoulder and the chestpiece that guarded his body to the thick plates that covered each arm and leg. It had been crafted in the forges of the finest smiths in the galaxy and like many creations of the dwarvish race was almost unparalleled in the ingenuity of its engineering. Beneath its outer shell were systems designed to interface with and enhance the technology built into both its wearer and the weapon he carried.

His rifle had originally been built for a sniper tasked with deposing the king of an alien race. Its design was bespoke – long, clean lines that spoke to efficiency of action being given priority over aesthetics – and it had served several operators well before it had been passed to him.

Carrying the weapon in both hands, the armoured man started running in the direction the marines had gone.

There was a huge gap between the roof he was on and the next one along his route. It was two metres higher too. But he did not stop running. Instead he ran faster and jumped, the power in his suit adding to that in his enhanced muscles, and he was propelled upwards. He engaged the jetpack built into the armour for just a second, firing it just long enough to give him the boost he needed, and landed, still running, on the elevated roof.

He was visible now but it did not matter. The marines were some way ahead of him and their attention was fully on the Veer-myn gang still artfully teasing them along another slightly broader alley. As big as he was, as incongruous as his presence was, the marines would never see him, just as they were not seeing the second gang of Veer-myn Stalkers moving on a parallel path to their right.

He saw them all though.

He stopped running and pulled up a simple map of the city on a projector built into his right wrist. With a command tapped in by his other hand he then superimposed over it the paths the three units he was now tracking. A quick zoom out and a scan of the surrounding streets and he could see it – the obvious kill box was just ahead and the marines were heading straight for it.

He switched off the map and turned the display over to a communications screen. He typed a short message and sent it out as a rapid burst transmission. It would be too short to be noticed by any unintended listeners and too deeply encrypted to be understood any time soon. But the rest of his team would receive it and they would be able to read his location and his orders for them.

Storm clouds were gathering in the sky above him as he set off again towards the marine unit.

The squad had followed the gang of Veer-myn deep into the streets of Guiders City until they found themselves on the edge of an open space, faced on three sides by two-storey buildings and on the fourth by the building that had given the place its name. King had recognised it immediately – Almar Square.

The square had been intended as an informal meeting place for the city, a communal area filled with flower beds and exotic trees in ornamental containers. A place where the hard-working employees of the nearby corporate enterprises could take a break from their businesses and relax together.

Carved stone benches lay along paths across the square and at the centre of it all was an extravagant metal sculpture built within what had once been a flowing fountain.

The sculpture was an abstract design and though King could not recall the name of its creator he remembered being told as a boy it was intended to represent man's journey into the stars, his never-ending quest for exploration, exploitation, and wealth. The young King had always thought it looked more like someone had simply welded together several long lengths of twisted scrap metal, leftovers perhaps from a nearby construction project, and then planted them in the middle of a circular duracrete pond before being paid an obscene amount of megacredits for their effort. The fountain and the pool around it was dry now though and the flower beds and lawns were filled with only cracked and dry soil.

On the far side of the square stood the imposing duracrete structure of the Acreon headquarters of Almar Incorporated. The building had been built and intended to coordinate interstellar traffic passing in and out of the Euxine sector. The arrival of one of the biggest frontier logistics corporations in the GCPS had been seen as a major vote of confidence in the planet and its administrators, so much so that the square it fronted onto had been renamed from 'Founder's Place'. Even when it had become obvious Acreon was not going to be 'the next big thing', that there were safer worlds with more hospitable biospheres in neighbouring systems, Almar had stayed, letting their building serve instead as a local administrative centre for Guiders and the various algae harvesting and inland mining operations still trying to turn a profit on the planet.

Now the building stood as a testament to the destruction the Veer-myn had caused on the day of their arrival.

When the cargo freighter CSS Hilton SP pulled into orbit almost directly above Guiders City, a few weeks before Drakenhof Marine had arrived, she was completely unannounced and unexpected. She had still barely raised an eyebrow at the city's space-traffic control centre. Vessels like the Hilton often made stops along their route for resupplies or to allow their crew to get some authentic gravity time in air that hadn't been recycled a thousand times. Even when the new arrival made no voice contact with the ground it was not seen as completely unusual. There was really no need for the crews of incoming ships to actually talk to anyone when they arrived at a modern port. Automated satellite systems handled the exchange of security and ID codes and arranged any requests for berthing services or crew transports, and the Hilton's on-board computer had broadcast her codes in a timely fashion. The human operator who logged the Hilton's arrival in orbit assumed that either her crew would eventually wake up from their artificially-maintained hibernation and request a transfer planetside, or the ship would simply break orbit once its computer had calculated the next safe slide point to continue its journey. Neither eventuality came to pass. Instead, the Hilton began to launch its compliment of cargo pods towards the planet's surface.

The pods had landed across the city, their inbuilt guidance systems bringing them down from orbit and their flaring arrestor jets slowing them enough for their deadly cargo to survive the journey. It was those jets that had started the fires that had burned so much of Guiders, but it was the hundreds of Veer-myn stumbling out of the crashed pods that caused the real chaos of the day.

The Almar building had taken an almost-direct hit from one of the wayward cargo pods. The impact had destroyed much of its facade and caused its first two floors to collapse almost completely into the square before it. Fire from the pod's jets had gutted the remainder of the building, the automated fire suppression systems yet another casualty of the pod that had landed on top of the city's desalination plant earlier in the attack.

The cargo pod was still in place, laying half-in and half-out of the shell of the building it had struck and resting on of the shallow slope of rubble that spilled down and out into the square itself. The bent lip of a satellite communications dish could be seen poking out from beneath what was left of its pale ceramic heat-shield and its long metal sides were blackened and dented. Ironically, the remains of an Almar corporate logo was just legible beneath all the dirt.

Its forward loading ramp, from which nearly a hundred raging Veer-myn had descended when the pod came to rest, lay open like the tongue of a giant metal beast, its interior a darkened cave.

But, of the Veer-myn they had been chasing, there was no sign.

The marines' pace slowed as they realised they had lost their quarry and the haste that adrenaline had fuelled began to be replaced by caution as the men scanned the buildings around them, looking for their next move.

"Where the hell'd they go?" said Stromer.

"We were right on them." said Thole. "Stay sharp, people."

The sun had almost set behind them as the marines spread out, searching for a sign of the Veer-myn they had been so close to catching just moments earlier.

King looked around the square, seeing the high walls and empty windows all around him, looking down on them all like blank, vacant faces. The storm he had sensed coming was almost on top of them now and flashes of lightning created stark shadows.

About halfway along the square to his left he could see a pedestrian pathway running between two buildings. At its mouth, it was easily wide enough for three or four people to walk side by side. As he drew nearer though, the lightning flashed again. In an instant, he saw the passage was blocked halfway along by a pile of rubble, higher than he or any of the others could quickly climb.

"Subway over here." Stromer said. He was standing on the far side of the square to King, shining the flashlight attached to the barrel of his weapon down what seemed to be a wide flight of stairs. "It's blocked though. They couldn't have gone this way."

King found a similar set of steps a few metres further along his side too and a sign above them that despite the layer of dirt and soot he recognised as a list of nearby street names. These stairs were also blocked by chunks of dura-crete and broken metal.

He stepped back and took another look at the blocked pedestrian pathway. There was something wrong about what he was seeing. As he looked up at the buildings on either side of it, he realised what that something was – neither building appeared damaged, at least not enough to create the pile of debris between them.

Ammit was a few metres behind him and was pulling out the digital map reader from his pack. King walked slowly towards him as he thumbed the safety on his launcher to the 'Armed' position, looking again at the empty shell of the Almar building and the vacant windows all around them. The weapon beeped its readiness.

"Sir, I think we ought to –"

But before King could finish his warning, the Veer-myn sprang their trap.

From behind them, from the direction by which the marines had entered the square, came a long and terrifying screech. The high-pitched noise echoed from the stony faces of the buildings around them. Then came an answering screech, this one slightly different in tone, sounding almost like a hooting, crowing noise that repeated three times.

Thunder cracked overhead.

"Everybody move!" yelled King.

The square was suddenly filled with what sounded like a hundred shrieks, all of them answering the first with the strange animalistic pattern. On the rooftops and in the windows of the buildings surrounding them appeared dozens of Veer-myn faces with long animal snouts and dark eyes.

"Combat pairings, people. Look sharp!" shouted Sergeant Thole. The marines were already moving into a rough circle, their weapons pointed towards the nearby buildings.

"Back out!" ordered Ammit. But before the platoon could take another step, the Veer-myn opened fire. Waves of sickly yellow energy bursts pulsed down into the square in a deadly crossfire. The marines scattered.

Stiller and Oneyul went down almost immediately, the sniper grunting as a beam of energy struck her on the thigh and Stiller crying out in pain as several shots struck him from different angles.

Oneyul dropped to one knee, her face contorted with pain, but she waved off Thole as he moved to help her. "I can make it," she shouted. Thole nodded and lifted his weapon, aiming it towards the leering face of a Veer-myn in a nearby window. He opened fire, sending a stream of shots at his enemy, forcing it to duck back into cover.

King ran over to where Stiller lay, face down and still, and rolled him over onto his back as more Veer-myn rays crackled through the air all around him. His partner was already dead though. Most of the rays that hit him had been absorbed by his armourweave plates, but at least one had gotten through. A small curl of smoke rose from an unarmoured point between the plates in Stiller's left side.

The rest of the unit had recovered from the shock of being caught in the Veer-myn ambush and were firing back, moving into their two-man fire-teams to protect each other and better concentrate their fire on the enemy. Nearly a dozen Veer-myn died quickly, their bodies falling limply from the rooftops around the square or simply dropping back out of sight. For a moment King thought they might be able to fight their way out of Almar Square.

But then Thole, the veteran sergeant, cried out as a shot hit him, the kinetic energy of it dropping him to his knees before he fell forwards, killed by an unseen Veer-myn shooter. King heard another voice; he thought it was Rains, yelling that he had been hit too. And he could hear Ammit trying to shout out orders amidst the chaos, trying to get his marines to move back towards the alley they had first used to enter the square. But when King looked that way he could see the silhouettes of more enemy shapes already moving into the square along it.

Their only exit was cut off and he could see only one option remaining to the unit.

"Into the fountain!" King shouted.

He grabbed Stiller's rifle and pulled the spare ammo pack from the dead man's belt. Then he ran as fast as he could to the ornamental pond at the square's centre before throwing himself over its lip. He grunted as he landed heavily on the hard floor on the other side, grateful it was at least dry, before hauling himself back up to cover the rest of the unit.

The other marines followed him in. They ran and crawled across ground that seemed to be alive with enemy fire and, like King had before them, threw themselves over the wall. It was only a low shelter, barely a metre high all around, but it was solid duracrete and the best cover in the square.

Enemy laser fire scorched the air around them, ricocheting noisily off the lip of the pond and the sculpture behind them, and the square was filled with the sound of hissing and screeching. King peeked over the edge of the unit's new home to see a wave of Veer-myn emerge on foot from the shadows of the Almar building, skittering down the slope of rubble and over the wrecked cargo pod towards their human prey.

They were humanoid, with two arms and legs and were roughly the same height as the marines, but there was something distinctly bestial about them too. They stood on legs with an extra joint below the knee, giving them both an almost goat-like appearance and the ability to move astonishingly fast. Their skulls were elongated with rat-like snouts and their mouths were filled with sharp, yellow teeth. Their arms were furred in shades of greasy brown and dirty grey with great tufts of it around their joints and at the base of their long, pointed ears. Each of them had a long, pale tail that flexed behind them, aiding their balance as they ran and jumped from cover to cover.

Most of them were what he had heard described as 'Night-crawlers', the lowest caste of their alien society. They were its foot-soldiers, its grunts, but there was little uniformity or appearance of professionalism amongst them. Most of them were clad in rags under rusted and primitive-looking metal plate armour that seemed to have been bolted onto their upper bodies, leaving their lower legs free to move. A few wore helmets, just as roughly crafted, but others went bare-headed or wore goggles that glinted in the flashes of weapons' fire.

As improvised as their armour appeared though, King had to admit it seemed effective. The unit was firing back now and he saw several shots bounce harmlessly off the oddly curved carapaces the aliens wore. Though the Veer-myn sometimes stumbled under the impact, they often jumped straight back up again too.

Their weapons shared the same home-made, outlandish aesthetic. Most of the 'crawlers carried the laser weapons colloquially known amongst the marines as 'ray-guns' – bulb-ended carbines and pistols that fired scatterings of odd-looking streams of yellow energy. But as savage and alien as they were in appearance, there was no denying they had outmanoeuvred the marines completely.

As the storm built overhead, the remaining marines made their stand.

CHAPTER 4

They were reacting exactly as he had thought they would. When the Drakenhof unit had realised their error, that they had run straight into an ambush, they had had not panicked as some soldiers might when faced with such a dire situation. Instead, they had done what their training would have told them to – find a defensible position and hold it. Eventually they would probably try to fight their way out again. But their enemy was too smart and too savage to simply let them back out of their mistake.

The marines were tough, but they had no idea what they were dealing with. They did not know how many Veer-myn they would have to kill to get out of their current position alive, nor did they know that there was not another friendly unit within a kilometre of them. No friendly units other than his.

A signal icon blinked to life on the display in his helmet's visor. His team was ready and in position and were awaiting a go order.

He scanned the battlefield, the advanced sensor package in his armour parsing data gathered by the scanners on the side of his helmet and automatically picking out targets across the battlespace, marking them with triangular red threat icons. For some of them it also projected vectors, likely movements and power level of their weapons, all the data he needed to see the flow of the battle.

A new group of icons began to flash more urgently off to his right. It was the gang of Veer-myn Stalkers that had shadowed the marines since the Buy-M-All. They were metres away from the square and would likely make their attack imminently. He knew it was possible the Drakenhof troops would not be able to survive this added onslaught.

But it was still not the right time to move.

"Hold." he said. "Not yet."

King fired Stiller's rifle as fast as he could. Accuracy felt less important than simply putting out enough shots to keep the enemy's heads down. Rains, Stromer, and the rest of the platoon were spread out around the lip of their improvised redoubt, firing in as many directions as they could and hoping against hope they could hold it. Of the ten marines who had entered Almar Square bare minutes earlier, only eight had made it into the relative safety of the fountain and most of them were hurt or bleeding. King himself had felt the armourweave plate on his back soak up the energy of a hit. It had felt like being smacked hard by someone holding a small hammer, but he was still alive.

Niles sat next to King with her back to the wall, a thick trail of blood running down the side of her face from beneath her helmet. She had been hit in the shoulder too and her left arm hung uselessly by her side, more blood slowly dripping from the cuff of her uniform onto the dry bed of the fountain. With her other hand she was working

42

the comm-link on her chest, trying to make contact with Sword. If the marines were going to survive Almar Square they all knew they would need support, either by air or by ground. But it was no use.

"Anything?" shouted Ammit. The lieutenant was trying to change the ammo pack on his rifle as fast as he could but King could see the new officer's hands were shaking.

Niles shook her head.

"Keep trying." Ammit said.

The marine nodded, her face pale, and keyed the comm-link on her chestplate again.

The fact she could not make contact with the unit's commanders, safely nestled in their bunker at Sword base nearly three kilometres away, was not a surprise, nor was it her fault.

As someone who had grown up on Acreon, King knew the desert winds were no laughing matter and the chalk-like sand of the plains north of Guiders were quite capable of ruining almost any technology. The storms that frequently rolled in from the desert rarely brought rain either, but were always highly-charged with static electricity that played havoc with the marines' comms. The lightning flashing above Almar Square would make calling in other units almost impossible.

There was another theory regarding the company's technical difficulties on Acreon though, one that was quite popular amongst the men and women in the non-comm barracks of Sword base. It had been suggested that the Veer-myn themselves were disrupting the radio comms, as and when they wanted to, with an as-yet undiscovered jamming technology.

King was no technician but, like most of the citizens

of the GCPS, he had a low opinion of the Veer-myn and their capabilities. As another volley of dirty yellow laser fire smacked into the wall he was kneeling behind, pinned along with the rest of his unit, smart Veer-myn were starting to feel like a much more credible idea.

"Incoming!" yelled Oneyul. She had set her rifle to fire single high-power shots, and she turned from picking off the 'crawlers firing down from the nearby rooftops to shooting the gang approaching from the alley at their rear.

They were Stalkers, the close-combat specialists of the Veer-myn nest. They launched themselves out of the alley's mouth brandishing savagely curved knives in their clawed fists, and sprang across the open ground towards the marines' redoubt. They moved so fast, leaping from side to side and skittering around the scant cover within the square that it was almost impossible to tell how many of them the marines were facing.

They barked and snapped as they ran, flecks of spittle flying from their wide-open mouths, their eyes glittering with a savage bloodlust.

King threw down his borrowed rifle and brought his BG-03M to bear. The drum-feeder whirred and the electronic primer whined as it sent a quick volley of rounds flying into the oncoming Veer-myn. These Veer-myn were more lightly armoured, choosing speed over protection. The rounds flew straight, each one exploding at chest-height amidst the surging mass of Stalkers. The booming explosions were mixed with blood-curdling shrieks as a dozen were quickly cut down. Arms, legs, and tails were sent flying through the air as bodies disintegrated into pink mist.

As devastating as King's fire had been, it was not quite enough. Five of the rampaging Stalkers made it through the

44

fusillade of defensive fire and leaped at the fountain wall. While the marines on one side of the position fired their weapons and did their best to keep back the Veer-myn coming from the Almar building, those behind them engaged in a vicious hand-to-hand melee.

King had dropped his launcher and pulled his combat knife from its sheath at his hip. He struck out at the nearest Veer-myn as it jumped across the lip of the fountain towards him, a jagged knife held high above eyes that glowed with an almost insane fervour.

The weight of the thing nearly knocked King down when it hit him. It stank of unwashed animal flesh and sweat-matted fur and its jaws snapped together inches from his face. He pushed back though, gripping its wrist with one hand and stabbing at it with his own weapon in the other. His revulsion gave his blows more strength and the long blade sunk deeply into the Veer-myn's soft unarmoured belly. It screeched with pain as the blade went in and King stabbed it again before throwing the mortally wounded alien away from himself.

Vallow was down, on his back and wrestling with another Stalker as it tried to impale him on its blade. On the other side of him King could see Stromer was battering another one down with the butt of his rifle, driving the weapon's stock repeatedly into its skull, grunting with the effort of each attack.

King swung his booted foot heavily into the midriff of the Veer-myn on top of Vallow and felt a crunch as the thing's ribs shattered. The creature squealed but it was not done, and it hissed again at its intended victim, a spray of thick spittle flying into Vallow's face. But then Stromer was on it, clubbing the monster across the back of its skull and a

45

spray of bright red blood erupted from its long snout. It slumped forwards, stunned by the blow, and King kicked it again. This time it fell sideways, dropping its knife as it sprawled out beside Vallow. Stromer switched the grip on his rifle and shot the Veer-myn through the back of its skull, a single shot instantly ending its life in a spray of skull fragments.

King heard someone yelling fiercely behind him and he turned to find Ammit, on his knees, repeatedly driving his own knife into the belly of another Stalker. Lying across the lip of the fountain beside him lay the body of the last of the assaulting gang, clearly dead with a long bloody gash running most of the way down its back. The lieutenant's upper body and legs were covered in blood, bright red and glistening wetly, but it was impossible to tell whether it was his or his enemy's.

King stooped and grabbed Ammit's wrist and the lieutenant's wide eyes locked with his.

"It's ok." King said. Both men were panting with exertion but King knew they would need calm heads if they were going to survive the battle.

"It's ok," he repeated. "You did it. But now we have to get out of here."

The assault was over, but there were still more Veer-myn pushing towards them from the ruins of the Almar building and over the wrecked cargo pod. King released the lieutenant's arm as he saw recognition come back into his eyes.

"Yeah, ok." said Ammit, wiping a trail of blood from his cheek and, in the process, making it much larger. He reached out and picked up his rifle from where it lay on the ground nearby and looked around as if seeing Almar Square for the first time.

"Ok," he said again. He was still breathing hard and, like all of them, was drenched in a layer of sweat, blood and dust. But he looked like a man who was thinking again, trying to figure a way out of the situation he and his marines were in.

"Good work, people," shouted Ammit as more Veer-myn fire sizzled through the air around him. "But we're not out of this yet." He stood and turned to face the now empty alley, the one they had used to enter the square barely minutes earlier. "Now how about we get the hell out of here?"

A streak of lightning crackled overhead and for a moment the entire square was lit up like an old black and white photographic rendering. But then, with a noise like a thousand electrified nails being dragged across a chalkboard, a sparking line of green fire arced out of the shadows at the base of the Almar Building. Ammit didn't even have time to turn around before the beam struck him in the middle of his back. The entirety of his armourweave plate was burned away in an instant and then so too was the flesh beneath. Ammit's agonised cry was cut short as the energy ray erupted from his chest, leaving a smoking hole where his heart and lungs had been.

The smell of burned flesh filled the marines' redoubt and Ammit's corpse dropped to its knees before slumping forward onto the creature he had just killed.

A new red icon winked to life in the observer's visor. A prime target had been identified and his armour's sensors were advising him to take immediate action.

He zoomed in the optics on his rifle, adjusting it to show him exactly what had been detected.

It was at the base of the building the Veer-myn had

used to mount their attack, skulking in the shadows of the ground floor. He could see its outline, rendered in red by his visor, standing taller than the Nightcrawlers and Stalkers it had sent out into the open to fight for it. He could see the shape of the heavy weapon it carried on its shoulder, the one it had just used to kill one of the marines in the square, the large batteries on its back and the heavy goggles that, he assumed, protected its eyes from the glare of discharging so much energy so fast. But when he switched the vision mode of his helmet to standard, the thing's shape was mostly obscured by the ruined cargo pod that lay across the entrance to the building. He did not have a clear shot.

He keyed on his subvocal communicator.

"Staker, confirm your position."

A green icon flashed up on his visor and he tracked it over to the other side of the square, on the top floor of the building facing the one he was crouching on.

"Confirm target identity."

Almost immediately he received an answer to his query.

"Confirmed. Prime target."

The observer made his decision.

"Good. Then we go now. Mouse, begin your run. Staker, prepare a tag round, please. Synchronised assault. Countdown begins at ten on my mark – mark."

The order given, the observer sighted his weapon again on the broken building.

"Let's see how you like this." he muttered.

CHAPTER 5

"Everybody down now!"

King dived to the ground and crawled over to the marines crouching facing the Almar building. He had retrieved Stiller's rifle and he flicked over its sights to night-vision mode. He cautiously placed the rifle on the lip of the fountain and aimed it towards where he thought the shot that had killed Ammit had come from. In the warm red glow of the weapon's optics he could see them now.

Deep within the building's ground floor was a small group of Veer-myn that were different to all those they had fought so far. There were three of them, each slightly larger than the Nightcrawlers and Stalkers and wearing heavier body armour too. Two carried wrist-mounted weapons with large-bore barrels, linked by thick tubes to heavy metallic canisters they wore strapped to their backs. He could see the animal faces of two of them, their eyes gleaming in the light being collected by his rifle's optics. But no, that wasn't quite right, he realised. One of them was scarred across its right cheek, its left ear a tattered stub as if it had suffered a serious injury in its past, and it had some kind of synthetic eyepiece or monocle in place of its natural eye.

The largest of the three seemed to be the boss of them all. It wore some kind of protective headgear over its head with large round lenses and the weapon it carried on one shoulder resembled a larger version of the Veer-myn ray-guns. In King's infra-red sight, the firing aperture of the heavy ray-gun glowed brightly with slowly dissipating heat.

"What the hell is it?" whispered Rains.

"Some kind of officer?" King said.

Oneyul was kneeling next to Rains and she aimed her own rifle in the same direction as King.

"It's a Malignus. One of their technician caste." she said. King and Rains stared at her.

"What?" she said. "I read the briefing files too."

"Whatever it is, it doesn't seem to be in a hurry to finish us off." Beggs whispered.

King scanned the ground between the marines and the Almar building and it was littered with the corpses of dead Veer-myn. But he could see no more Nightcrawlers attempting to rush the marine position. He caught a few fleeting glimpses of movement around near the cargo pod but nothing was now trying to cross the square itself. Even the Veer-myn that had been firing down at them from the windows of the nearby buildings had disappeared. The only noise in the square was that of the storm blowing above them; the steady patter of sand falling down.

He looked back, towards the only unblocked exit he knew from Almar Square. It looked close, temptingly so. Close enough that a fit, uninjured marine could likely make it at a sprint.

"Who cares what the hell it is?" Stromer whispered, "Let's get out of here while we can!"

The marine corporal started to rise towards the alley but King stopped him, reaching out a hand and pulling him back down inside the fountain.

"No! Wait," he said. "That's exactly what they want." King glanced back towards the Almar Building. "We're completely cut off out here and they know it. They've given up trying to rush us. Now they're just trying to flush us out. But if we run, they'll kill most of us before we even get to that alley back there. And those they don't they'll hunt down in the streets outside."

As if in response to King's analysis, the night was torn apart by the screeching sound of the Veer-myn heavy weapon firing again.

"Incoming!" shouted Vallow. The marines all ducked down, hugging the inside of the low stone wall of the fountain. The blast from the heavy ray-gun screamed overhead, clipping the side of the huge statue behind them. There was an odd crackling sound and the air was filled with a smell like leaking batteries as the metal super-heated and began to buckle.

The beam cut out then and a few strands of the most expensive piece of art on Acreon began to slowly sag, dragged out of shape under the planet's gravity. King could hear the metal popping and pinging as it cooled again.

Stromer was the first to get back to his feet and he sighted his rifle over the wall towards the Almar building.

"Looks like it's reloading or something." he said. He turned back to King. "So what's the plan then? How are going to get out of this?"

King looked at the unit's other corporal, a surprised look on his face. But then it hit him. With the sergeant and Ammit both dead, he was technically the senior officer in the squad. He had joined up with Drakenhof a full three months before Stromer.

The others were looking at him now too, expectant looks on their tired and bloodied faces. Even the normally taciturn Beggs was looking at him with narrowed eyes beneath the brow of his helmet.

King cursed and wiped the sweat from his forehead as he weighed up the options. They could not get back out of the square. But they could not stay where they were either.

There was only one thing they could do.

He turned to Oneyul.

"Hey, Oneyul, that story about the Marauder, how much truth is in that?"

The sharpshooter looked over at him, a faint smile on her lips.

"It's true enough," she said.

"Ok, then. Well that makes you our fire support tonight. Vallow, you're coming with us."

"Ok," Oneyul's partner said. "Where we going?"

King took a deep breath.

"Straight down their throats. Look. If we stay here, we die. If we run, we die. I don't like either of those choices. So I say we go the other way, finish what we started. Maybe take a few of those bastards with us. I've got three rounds left in the BG-03. We'll use them as cover and I'll take Vallow and Stromer up the left flank. Beggs, Rains, you go right. Oneyul, you keep them off us. Kill as many as you can until we get close enough to tear them apart. What do you say?"

Before anyone could answer though, the comm link on Niles's chest crackled to life. There was a burst of static and sharp squeal of feedback, then a voice.

"Marine patrol, Almar Square, come in."

"What the hell?" King shrugged at Stromer and took the comm link paddle from Niles.

"Er, this is the marine patrol." King said. Whoever was on their comms had not identified themselves or used any Drakenhof call-signs. "Who am I talking to?"

There was a moment of static and then the comm chirped to life again.

"Marine unit, I am inbound your location. Tell your men to get down."

King's eyes met Stromer's.

"I have no idea." said King.

Then, several things happened at once.

The storm was still blowing above them and lightning flashed. A peal of thunder rolled across the square but from somewhere above him and to his right King heard the sound of breaking glass. As the shards of whatever had just been broken fell to the ground inside the square a harsh screech came from the direction of the Almar building. King swivelled, bringing his rifle's sights to his eye and focusing on the Veer-myn boss with its heavy weapon. Only it was not holding the weapon any more. It had dropped the heavy ray-gun and seemed to be pawing at its chest, as if there were something stuck to its armoured chest it was trying to scratch off.

Suddenly the Almar Building was flooded with light and King felt a downdraft of air as something big, yet remarkably quiet, hovered into the air above the marines. He lowered his weapon and shielded his eyes as he looked up, trying to identify what exactly it was.

Lightning flashed again and he caught the outline of whatever it was silhouetted against the brightness. It was a military aircraft, that much was obvious from its thick armoured shell, but other than that the design was unfamiliar. It was too big to be a Hornet and besides, King guessed they would have heard the triple-rotors of a TAD-65 coming at them from kilometres away. As manoeuvrable and agile as the Hornet was, he could not imagine many marine pilots flying them with anything like the precision required to come down to a hover inside a heavily built-up area like Almar Square. Its body was bulky, like a transporter of some kind, but he could also see two huge laser cannons mounted alongside missile pods to hard points on the undersides of its wings.

He looked back towards the Veer-myn. They seemed stunned, frozen in place by the harsh white light coming from the aircraft's nose. Their surprise only lasted a second at most, but it was long enough.

The spotlight winked out but the dark interior of the square was instantly lit again as the aircraft's cannons opened fire. To the marines below the noise was almost deafening and King could feel the heat of each blast. He didn't want to imagine what it felt like to be at their receiving end.

The shots whipped into the Almar Building's open front and the Veer-myn there were instantly atomised, their bodies turned to a fine mist whenever the huge beams struck them. Clouds of debris and rubble flew up into the air as the aircraft strafed the front of the Almar building.

Then it was the rocket pods' turn to fire and the marines hugged the ground beneath them as it shook with each impact. Salvoes of fiery projectiles streaked towards the far end of the square killing even more Veer-myn. The Nightcrawlers that had been preparing to overrun the marines were blasted out of their hiding places and ripped apart by flying shrapnel.

"Get down!" King yelled as he grabbed Rains, pulling the rookie marine down behind the fountain's wall. A flaming missile had struck the cargo pod almost exactly in its centre and the explosion sent shards of hot metal flying across the square, cutting down the last of the Veer-myn as they tried to flee the destruction.

When it was over, when its munitions had been expended and there was nothing left still moving at the Veer-myn's end of the square, the mysterious aircraft's engines let out a growl of power before it lifted its nose and turned away from the battlefield, disappearing over the buildings to the marines' right.

King looked up. The storm overhead had cleared and he could see the first few stars of the night appearing between the clouds.

"What. The hell. Was that?" Stromer's face was a picture of stunned confusion as he picked himself up from the dusty floor. Moments earlier, he like all of them had been facing imminent death, certain that at any moment they would either be overrun and torn apart by the Veer-myn or die trying to charge them down. Now, instead, he was still standing and it was the Veer-myn that had been destroyed.

King stood and then helped Stromer up. They were both covered with dust and debris, but they were alive. He looked over towards the last place he had seen the aircraft before it departed.

"I know what it was." Rains said from behind them. "The Council has sent us help."

King was still watching the sky.

"Well that's the last thing we need." he said. "Council be damned."

***

55

The air in the square was hazy with the after-effects of so much energy being discharged so quickly in tight quarters. It tasted of ozone and new flames crackled around the blasted shell of the cargo pod. Most of the marines were picking themselves up, pulling themselves back together and helping each other patch up their wounds and sucking down whatever was left in their hydration bladders. There were no more Veer-myn left to fight – those that hadn't been killed by the unknown aircraft had fled in its wake. Now it was time to recover.

Rains was coughing, retching as he threw up what was left of his last meal over the side of the fountain. Beggs sat next to him, a patient smile on his face as he waited for his partner to get it out. When he sat up, his face was covered with a thick mix of blood, dust, and dirt. Beggs looked appraisingly at the rookie.

"Now you're not so shiny." he whispered.

For King, the adrenaline was wearing off. The high of combat, of being on the edge of life and death, was being replaced by the awareness of what he had just survived. He could feel his limbs starting to shake a little as the sane part of him, the part him that had to be buried or put to sleep for a while in order to survive bloody combat, caught up with the reality of the situation.

He looked at his hands. He was sure he had been wearing gloves when he had left Sword Base a few hours earlier. At some point in the desperate fight for survival in Almar Square he must have taken them off. The skin of his hands was dark now, completely covered in a layer of grime and dried blood. Only some of it was his.

"So what now, top?"

It took King a moment to recognise the voice as Stromer's

and another to realise he was addressing him.

He undid the chinstrap of his helmet and scratched the stubble growing under it. Sword Base was a long way to walk, particularly carrying dead and wounded.

"We'll have to split up," he said. "I'll take two with me, see if we can get clear of all this." He gestured around himself at the tall buildings that surround them. "See if we can get a link to Sword. Call in some backup."

He was about to ask for volunteers to stay behind and guard the unit's dead when something made him stop. He wasn't sure what exactly. He didn't exactly hear anything, it was more of a feeling, a feeling of a presence somewhere nearby.

Quickly he dropped to one knee, grabbing for the rifle he had left on the fountain bed and intending to come around with it ready to fire.

But instead, as he gripped the stock, he felt something heavy slam down onto the weapon's barrel, jarring it from his hand and pinning it to the ground. He let out a yelp as the impact twisted his wrist and, somewhat unbalanced, he scrabbled backwards and away from the apparition that had disarmed him.

It was as if the night had come alive. The darkness itself seemed to ripple and bulge as something huge moved through it. It was hard to look at – King got the feeling that this thing, whatever it was, only got harder to see the more you tried to focus on it.

He heard a muffled gasp and he looked back, over his shoulder to see Oneyul still sitting on the lip of the fountain with her hands held up in the air. Another dark and blurry form had moved up behind her and now, somehow, was aiming her own rifle with its expensive Accutek scope directly at her head. It was almost as if the rifle were floating on air, being held by a phantom.

The rest of the team froze. None of them had their weapons at the ready and most looked too tired to put up much of a fight anyway.

"Please, there will be no need for that," said a voice from somewhere within the blur that had stepped on King's gun. Its shape seemed to shiver slightly then, like seeing something resolving through a haze of heat, before it resolved into a tall, heavily-armoured figure.

The armour was angular, grey, and unmarked and, they could all now see, had been wearing some kind of electronic camouflage cloak. As the cloak dropped to the ground, the faceplate of the newcomer's helmet retracted and folded in on itself in a series of small precise movements. Beneath it was a human face. It was male, broad and with high angular cheekbones. Even in the failing light of Acreon's evening, his eyes were bright and alert. He carried a long heavy rifle but, most importantly, he was smiling.

He bent over and retrieved King's rifle, the one he had fought with since retrieving it from Stiller, and, holding it by its barrel, extended it towards the corporal.

"My name is Roca." it said. "I'm here to help you."

The Mother hissed angrily. She was in a dangerous mood and all the brethren knew it.

She reclined on her birthing throne, her massive corpulent form elevated above the rest of the chamber and her assembled children, her tail lashing to and fro on the warm pile of furs and fabrics they had made for her. Her skin was pale and covered with a glistening sheen of sweat. Thick black veins showed through it across her massive abdomen and pulsed with her anger. Beneath the hanging lights of the chamber she bared her teeth at the leaders of her children as they abased themselves before her. She snapped at them with her long sharp fangs, loudly and savagely. She was beautiful to them and they loved her, but they had also failed her badly.

The war with the humans was not going well. It had not done so almost from the start. She had lost many litters, seen many of her children lose their lives fighting to save the nest, to hold off the outsiders that threatened everything she had built and worked for beneath the planet's surface. And now her breeding partner was gone too. Killed in the latest battle, leaving her with no-one with whom she could birth more pups.

The Brood Mother was old. She could feel it even if she did not express it.

She did not measure time the way others did. Other races, even her own children, might use arbitrary factors like the passing of sunsets or phases of the moon to keep track of time but to her these were irrelevant and passing things, either entirely dependent on what planet you were on or completely irrelevant if you were on a starship. So she measured time in terms of the number of litters she had produced, the number of partners she was coupled with. She measured time in lives, in children, real tangible things. And, as she saw her nest being destroyed, slowly whittled away in a war she did not ask for, she felt her time running out.

The Brood Mother surveyed the Maligni and gang-leaders arrayed before her, all of them bowing down and inclining their heads slightly to show their throats, to show her fealty and loyalty. She hissed at them again but this time more quietly. She was listening.

Beside her, almost completely obscured by her bulk, her latest litter wriggled restlessly. It would need to feed soon, she knew that. But first it wanted to talk to her.

It did not speak with a voice anyone else could hear. The mix of growls and screeches and pheromones most of her kind used was a language it did not know. Instead, it spoke to her directly, whispering into her head. Sometimes it had one voice, quiet and insistent. Sometimes it was a chorus. She listened to its small voice now as she took the measure of the Maligni before her.

She knew what they were thinking, what they cared about – their machines. Their own creations, the things they made in the darkest hidden places of the nest, their workshops and laboratories. Many of them had been destroyed in the long war and they wanted to go back to their workshops now and build more machines for her, for the nest. She would let them, she knew they would need them.

But the quiet voice whispered something different to her. It told her that no amount of war machines would be enough. That no amount of litters would save her or the nest. It told her that something far more drastic would be needed if she and all her children were not to die on this world they had made their home.

The war was escalating and to match the growing threat she would need to do something radical.

The answer to her problems, the voice told her, was in this very chamber.

The Mother's eyes had become glazed and unfocused, the flames of her fury turning to smouldering embers, and while she was distracted many of the lesser brethren had taken the opportunity to skulk out of her throne chamber.

The gangs of fighters disappeared into the network of tunnels that made up the nest leaving only the Maligni to face the Mother's wrath.

Suddenly her eyes refocused and the fire came back to them, though she was no longer releasing the pheromonal scent of anger that had set all her children's nerves on edge. She was drained by the experience of communing with her litter and she felt hunger gnawing at her insides. Her prodigious gut growled with emptiness. But she felt a kind of elation too.

She examined her remaining Maligni, looking each one over and dismissing them one by one with a low growl. They backed away from her gratefully, humbly. Soon there was only one left.

He was not the biggest of her children, perhaps not the cleverest either, but she knew he was a survivor. There was a white streak of scar tissue running from the stub of one ear all the way across his snout, a souvenir of his own time as a pup at her breast when he had fought for survival like all her children did. One of his eyes had been lost at some point in his youth too and he had replaced it with an artificial one, a collection of lenses bound together in metal in a way the Brood Mother did not care to understand. All she had to know was that he was capable of great viciousness if provoked. Or if it suited him. And her litter was telling him he was.

The last Malignus' eyes met hers and she heard a faint whirring as his artificial one focused on her face.

This one, the voice told her. *There is a weapon on this world that could win this war for us. This one knows where it is.*

CHAPTER 6

The Accuser raced across the black sky like a bad omen, its Xian-Seng engines firing twin plumes of thrust that easily made it the fastest thing on the planet.

The ship was at its base an Arbiter, a variant of the standard Accuser Interceptor model equipped with Polaris laser weaponry and high-grade targeting equipment to make it an expert tank-hunter and even a respectable dog-fighter. But it had also been extensively modified, according to its master's specifications, with sensor-dupers and engine baffles that could make it almost as hard to detect as he was.

More obviously, its fuselage had been widened and slightly extended in order to accommodate a larger passenger bay than those carried by Accuser dropships. It served not only as an assault transport, but as a mobile base of operations

Today it was being used as the emergency evac vehicle for the dead and wounded of Drakenhof Marine.

Sword Base had been built, like most human settlements so far from the architectural niceties of the Core, from a base of Shensig habtainers. The same massive crates that had been used to ferry in the men, women, vehicles, and material necessary to liberate Guiders and any other infested areas of Acreon, had been broken down and repurposed. They had been used to build two blocks of barracks, a mess, storehouses, maintenance sheds, a medical bunker, and a large, heavily fortified armoury and command bunker. An error by the planners who had put the mission package had been discovered a week after the force's arrival on Acreon. But such was the utility built into Shensig's tiles that the marines had been able to reuse sections from an abandoned building on the outskirts of Acreon to finish the third barracks block.

The original shuttleport around which Sword had been constructed was nearly two kilometres from the outskirts of Guiders. It had never been completed and only had one functioning landing pad so Drakenhof had added two more, one for each of the TAD-65 Hornet dropships the company had allocated to the Acreon mission. The two new pads were both elevated and the whole compound was surrounded by a high bulwarked wall, also constructed from Shensig tiles, but reinforced with the same heavily armoured upgrades that had been used to fortify the command bunker.

Even so, the ubiquity of Shensig's architectural boon to the galaxy was such that, at a distance at least, Sword Base might have passed for any number of corporate structures across the known galaxy. Unless, of course, one considered the armed guards patrolling its perimeter and the four heavy 'Equalizer' laser cannons, one mounted one on each corner guard tower.

A fifth tower stood at almost the direct centre of the compound, thick glass windows giving it a three-sixty degree view. It was the Air Traffic Control Tower, and within it the ATC officer on duty stood as he heard the roar of unexpected engines approaching the number three pad from the direction of Guiders City.

Three was the closest pad to the tower and to see it properly the ATC had to lean forwards across his console, taking care not to spill the mug of caffa he had brought from the machine on the floor below. He was just in time to see the nose of an unfamiliar and most definitely not Drakenhof-issued aircraft flare into a perfect landing at the centre of the floodlit pad.

The craft's running lights were illuminated and exhaust gases were venting along its lower hull as it settled onto the deck. The ship was painted a flat grey over black sections with two red stripes across its wings, angled to form a broad 'V' across its back. Other than that, it was unmarked.

Back in his seat, the ATC hurriedly flicked through a dozen confirmation screens on his pull-up display. Somehow, without him even being aware it was happening, the unexpected arrival had managed to pass every automated security challenge the tower computers had sent it in a matter of seconds. No, not passed, he realised – it had simply *overridden* them. Some screens showed the correct passwords and ident codes had been exchanged but other checks seemed to have been simply ignored. Instead of flagging the new arrival as an intruder and quickly blasting it out of the sky with the Equalizers, the usually reliably paranoid security system had disregarded it entirely. It was as if the ship he could see on the ground less than a hundred metres away simply did not exist.

But while the computer did not recognise the aircraft on pad three, the ATC was fairly sure *he* did.

He scrabbled for the emergency comm-link to the duty officer in the command bunker. As the link tried to connect he stood again and watched as the grey ship's rear loading ramp lowered smoothly to the ground and its passengers disembarked. Some of them he recognised. They were grunts but they wore Drakenhof uniforms.

He couldn't hear what was going on through the reinforced glass, but he could see one of the grunts shouting down from the pad. There were a gaggle of technicians and service staff lounging nearby, using the shelter of a stack of parts crates for an unofficial caffa break. One of the technicians immediately ran off towards the medical block while the others began to move towards the pad's access ramp.

By the time they got there the ATC was in his seat again, the communicator pad jammed between his chin and shoulder as he tried to make a note of the time of arrival of the new ship. Finally, someone picked up at the other end.

"Sir, this is the ATC on watch." he said. "Yes, sir. I thought you would want to know immediately – the Enforcers are here!"

They made a strange convoy, passing through the marine compound.

Roca, or to give him his full title, Lieutenant Commander Roca, Forward Observer of the Enforcers, was a giant, standing head and shoulders above most of the Sword Base personnel. Even without his rifle, armed only with his sidearm, he was an imposing figure. He moved like a predator on the hunt, his footsteps light and precise, but there was a nobility to him too, a sense of self-assurance and absolute confidence in his place and power.

Flanking him were the two Pathfinders he had chosen for Acreon, Sergeants Mouse and Staker. They were wearing only light reconnaissance armour over their camouflage fatigues, but neither looked any less dangerous. Pathfinders were the Enforcers' scouts and intelligence agents, often the ones tasked with the most dangerous missions given to the corps, and both were veteran warriors. They carried their weapons slung across their chests, and an assortment of grenades, close combat weapons, and pouches filled with more gear and ammunition hung from their webbing and belts.

Leading the trio from the landing pad, where medical orderlies and docbots were already dealing with the wounded marines was King, the marine corporal they had found trying to keep his men alive during the brief but bloody battle of Almar Square.

Roca guessed he and his team were probably the first Enforcers most of the onlookers at Sword Base had ever seen in the flesh. For most human beings, particularly those living this far out from the Core, the Enforcers were an almost abstract thing, as real as Asterians or black holes. Everybody knew they existed, that they were out there in the great wide galaxy somewhere, but most humans never actually saw them. Those that did often wished they had not.

The Galactic Co-Prosperity Sphere was, in spirit, a pan-galactic free market. From its beginnings on the first few habitable planets mankind had reached after leaving Old Earth it had grown, through a series of expansions, into the largest territory in the known galaxy. Within it, thousands of corporate bodies – companies, conglomerates, investment houses and numerous others – were all unified in the pursuit of claiming the riches of the galaxy for mankind. Some owned or had leases on entire planetary bodies and systems. Others were only locally organised. And, while the largest groups could claim to manufacture everything from bedsprings to rocket boosters, many were more specialised in the goods and services they offered. There were mining groups and shipping outfits, logistics specialists and biotech conglomerates. Every imaginable form of exploration, entertainment, and exploitation existed as a corporate venture somewhere within the GCPS. Over them all sat the Council of Seven.

Officially their role was administrative and most Councils since the inception of the GCPS had preferred their role to be seen as a benevolent one, benign even. But there had to be at least some order amidst the free-wheeling chaos of the corporations. Some decisions were simply too big to be handled in any kind of piecemeal process or according to parochial political priorities – it was that kind of thing that had doomed Old Earth, after all – and so the Council had the Enforcers.

The Enforcers were their private military force, an elite group shrouded in secrecy and equipped with the best arms and armour money could buy. Each one had gone through 'the program', an intensive course of biological and psychological reconstruction that turned the hardiest of recruits into humanity's most deadly fighting force. They were intended as the Council's last word on any subject, its final answer to any question, and the resolution to any debate.

Even amongst this elite group, Roca was something special.

He had been hand-picked by the Council themselves to serve as a Forward Observer, or FO, acting as their eyes and ears across the galaxy and reporting back what he found. It was his responsibility to identify and confront any and all threats to the GCPS, no matter what form they took or how much danger it placed him or his forces in. To achieve this, he had a great deal of operational freedom. He could go wherever he believed necessary to carry out his mission and had access to virtually any Enforcer resources he required.

The ability to handpick his team was, he believed, invaluable. Mouse and Staker were both highly regarded operators within the corps.

Mouse he had worked with before, first during several missions targeting a rogue faction of Marauders and then, sometime later, fighting a small corporation that had tried to defy the Council by pursuing ventures outside the areas it had been licensed to exploit. She had served in both ops with distinction, carrying out her duties with a cold precision and professionalism that had resulted in Roca marking her out as a potential future FO herself.

Staker he knew only by reputation. As an FO, there was little data in the GCPS Roca could not access directly. And yet, oddly, Staker's personnel file had some obvious omissions; encrypted and redacted sections that did not immediately recognise Roca's security codes. Roca had chosen not to pursue it further. If he took it up with the Council he knew it was likely that they would tell him what Pathfinder Sergeant Staker had done for them on the world of Tyrannus and amongst the rebel cells in the Sygnar Cluster. But he also knew that if they had sealed those records they would have only done so for good reason and Roca could do nothing but trust their judgment. Talking to other senior officers within the corps had also produced nothing but high recommendations for Staker and so Roca had selected him for Acreon.

And now, he had decided, it was time to meet the Drakenhof Commandant of that planet.

He did not have to. His authority as a representative of

the Council themselves was such that he could carry out his mission without so much as a by-your-leave to any planetary or corporate governance. He knew there were several other Forward Observers who would do just that – simply slide in, take their prize, and be back out before any local power could step in the way. He had done it himself a few times and it was quite possible he could fulfil or at least attempt to fulfil his mission on Acreon without any corporate assistance or interference. Staker, the more reclusive of the two Pathfinders, had advised as much. But it was in the man's nature to do things alone and Roca had a feeling there was more to Drakenhof than met the eye.

Something about their deployment maybe, or their tactics. He wasn't quite sure yet. But in all his time as an Enforcer he had not encountered a mission yet that wasn't better served by having more information supplied. As King led him and his team away from the landing pads, and past the armoury, Roca marked the layout of the camp almost automatically. The recording equipment in his helmet logged data about distances, the dimensions of the buildings they passed, the numbers of troops present, without him giving it a thought.

It was late, but the camp was still busy. He had identified barracks blocks in opposite corners of the camp as Mouse brought the Accuser in to land, and it seemed like most of their inhabitants had found reason to be somewhere along his team's route since they landed. They walked past the entrance to the camp's armoury and on to the heavy blast doors that opened into the command bunker. All the while they were being watched by groups of soldiers doing their best to look like casual observers. The news of his arrival had travelled fast.

King's attitude seemed very different to that of the other soldiers though. After he revealed his presence, Roca had gotten the impression that, if weren't for the clear need his men had for medical attention, Corporal King might have refused the offer of transportation back to Sword. Even then, as they had limped aboard the Accuser and Roca and Staker had handed out first aid and emergency supplies, King had barely said a word to either of them directly.

The awe, or rather the fear his uniform inspired had rankled with Roca when he had first joined the corps. He had become an Enforcer because he knew there were real monsters out in the darkness of space and he wanted to fight them. So, despite the reservations of those closest to him, he had volunteered for the program. As an Enforcer he knew he had probably saved more lives than most corporate citizens would believe possible. And yet they feared him.

But then there were times when fear could be very useful.

CHAPTER 7

In Roca's experience there were two types of senior military officer, and while he did not assign either any superiority of value, he was certainly more comfortable with one than the other.

The first type were the combat leaders, the kind of commanders who led their warriors from the front. Men and women who possibly could not actually fight a war from any other position. The Enforcers valued such leaders – insisted on them, in fact. Every rank of Enforcer, whether they be a team leader or a battlefield commander was trained to carry out their duties in armour and under fire. Roca himself was no stranger to commanding large numbers of his fellow warriors in battle.

The second type of leader were those whose gifts were better suited to the rear echelons of campaigns; the planners and administrators of warfare. Roca did not hold any prejudice against such officers. He was quite aware that although some soldiers simply weren't built for combat as such, their abilities to coordinate and manage a protracted campaign could still be a valuable gift to the fighting force they commanded. They simply weren't cut from the same cloth he was.

As soon as he saw him, Roca knew Drakenhof Marine Commandant Patrin fell into this second category of officer.

They found him in the command centre at the heart of the bunker. It was a large room with a low ceiling, filled with the noise of soldiers at work. A line of monitors extended almost all the way around it and beneath them were numerous workstations at which Drakenhof staff officers were engaged with coordinating their company's mission on Acreon.

None of them looked up as Roca's group entered the room.

The two Pathfinders took the opportunity to instantly fade into the background, instinctively finding the most shadowed positions at the room's rear, one on either side of the slowly closing security doors that guarded the room. Roca didn't have to look back to know that both of them, as incongruous as they were in a room filled with smartly-uniformed officers and military personnel, would be becoming as close to invisible as was possible without electronic aid. It was just how they were trained.

Patrin himself was poring over an actual paper map of Guiders City. He had it spread out over a large octagonal map table at the centre of the room that was lit from beneath, and appeared to be discussing notations he had made on it with one of his officers.

Patrin wore a Drakenhof field officer's uniform, high black leather boots over black trousers and a black tunic jacket. The jacket and trousers were both trimmed in the red of the company's owning house and Roca noted the full gold hawk device over the man's left breast that indicated actual membership of the ruling clan.

His face did not resemble the other Drakenhofs with whom Roca was familiar though. The Drakenhofs were an old and influential family and Roca had seen several members of their family lobbying the Council for political and legal support back in the Core. But while they had all been tall, thin, and possessed of sharp, almost aquiline features, Patrin was considerably shorter with full lips and cheeks and a small dimple in his chin.

But he definitely carried himself like a Drakenhof. He stood with one hand held behind his back, electronically signing with a wave of his other, chip-implanted wrist the datapads and order sheets being brought to him by junior staff, barely glancing up at each document. His attention was almost fully focused on the map laid out before him as he planned the liberation of Guiders.

With a sidelong glance towards Roca that seemed half-apology and half-accusation, Corporal King stepped forwards towards Patrin's table and snapped to attention.

"Sir, Corporal King, 3rd Platoon, reporting."

Patrin glanced up and matched King's salute with a shallower one of his own.

"Corporal. And you've brought company, I see."

"Sir, yes, I –" King seemed at a loss for words.

Roca stepped forwards and removed his helmet.

"Commandant Patrin, I am Lieutenant Commander Roca of the –"

"Yes, yes," interrupted Patrin. The commandant had stepped away from his map table and was regarding the Enforcer with cold hard eyes. "I know who you are, Lieutenant, and I know what you are. Welcome to Sword."

Roca was neither surprised nor particularly put out by

the frosty reception. But he would not be put off by it, nor would he reciprocate it. Drakenhof was not why he was on Acreon, after all. Both he and the mercenary company had a common enemy.

The officer standing beside Patrin wore a field uniform like King's, with armourweave plates over black combat fatigues. The rank insignia on the chest plate of his armour told Roca he was a major.

"I understand I have you to thank for bringing back my unit. At ease, Corporal." the major said.

Patrin smiled. "Lieutenant, allow me to introduce Major Corrick, my ranking field officer here on Acreon."

Roca nodded respectfully towards the major. This one looked more like a combat soldier. He wore his full armour, even while on base.

"Major," Roca said. "I'm glad we were able to be of assistance. It's why I'm here. But actually I have to thank them for aiding us."

"Oh? How so?" Corrick said.

Roca stepped forward and removed a small device from his belt. It was a palm-sized holo-projector and he placed it on top of the map of Guiders City before activating it. A two-dimensional display appeared above the table, a still image he had culled from the feed captured by cameras attached to the nose of the Accuser. It was a low-res image, made grainy by the lack of light in the square and the movement of the ship, but the front of the Almar Building could be clearly seen as well as the alien shapes of the Veer-myn within it.

"This is the target we were able to terminate this evening." Roca said. He tapped one of the Veer-myn figures within the image, causing the viewpoint of the hologram to shift as it zoomed in. It was the larger of the three 'leader' Veer-myn and although it was still in the shadows of the building, the heavy ray-gun was clearly visible on its shoulder.

"A Malignus?" said Corrick.

"Yes," said Roca. "One of their leader caste, their mechanics and inventors. But this was not just any Malignus. We believe this was fact one of the Progenitors of the nest here on Acreon."

"A Progenitor?"

Roca looked towards Patrin. "Yes, sir. The 'father' of the nest if you will."

Patrin looked sceptical. "I'm sorry, I was under the impression Veer-myn nests were matriarchal societies. Ruled by a single Brood Mother."

"Yes, that is correct." Roca said. "They are. And there may be dozens of Maligni working for them at any one time. But a few of them will be elevated further. They may still be employed building the nest's weaponry and technology, but they also procreate with the nest's female. As well as this, they are often tasked with leading the nest's warriors, its 'Nightcrawlers' and the like in battle. It is quite likely this creature," Roca gestured towards the holographic Veer-myn, "played a key part in the fight against your personnel throughout Guiders. Its termination, something that was only possible with the assistance of Corporal King and his men, will, I believe, significantly aid your mission to rid this world of the Veer-myn threat."

Corrick wore a long moustache and he smoothed it thoughtfully against his cheeks as he looked at the image of the Progenitor.

"But how can you be sure that this thing is what you say it is?"

Roca was tight-lipped. "My team and I have – special intelligence regarding these things."

Patrin smiled.

"What he means is that he and his team have been on Acreon for far longer than we would suspect, spying on the Veer-myn. And possibly us." he said. "But he cannot say this."

Roca said nothing but stepped forward and deactivated the projector, replacing it on his belt.

"Well." said Patrin. "Then again, we would certainly like to thank you and your team for your assistance." he said. "But I take it that with your mission here concluded you will be leaving straight away?"

Roca frowned.

"No," he said. "We will not. Although terminating the Progenitor is certainly a priority and, as I said, will likely aid in the liberation of this world, it is not the primary objective of my mission here."

"You have other business on Acreon?" asked the major.

"I do." Roca replied.

"And may I ask what that is?" Corrick said.

Roca smiled thinly. "You can ask, certainly. But I cannot tell you. Not at this point anyway. My mission is – classified. All I can say is that this is not the first world reporting unusual Veer-myn activity that I have visited in recent times. I am trying to find out why."

Patrin and Corrick glanced at each other. It was only a fleeting gesture, one that might have gone unnoticed except for Roca's heightened perception, but the two officers were clearly uneasy about something. Roca was getting the feeling it was more than just the usual outer-sphere suspicion of Enforcers.

Patrin folded his hands behind his back but he spoke with a diplomatic tone.

"Lieutenant Roca, I am sorry to say I think that puts us in a rather awkward position. You see, as much as we appreciate your intervention here this evening, I do not think we can allow you and your team to simply come and go as you please."

Roca raised an eyebrow at Patrin's choice of words.

"Allow?" he said.

"Yes," Patrin said. "Allow. Your presence here is simply not required. This is a legally sanctioned contract and all commercial and administrative rights have been temporarily ceded to the Drakenhof clan. That is to say, we own this world and we do not wish for any outside interference in our business here."

Roca spoke slowly and carefully.

"Commandant, let me assure you, we, I, have no interest in taking over your interests or your campaign here. I promise you, if the Council viewed it as necessary there would be far more than three Enforcers standing here now."

"No doubt." said Patrin.

"That said," Roca continued, "The Council does wish for me to be here. And that is why I will not be leaving until I choose to."

The Commandant waved a hand dismissively.

"Please, Lieutenant. Don't try to scare me with veiled threats. As I said before, I know what you are and where you come from and I know what you are capable of if you don't get your way." His eyes flickered down to the sidearm at Roca's hip – the Enforcer's hand rested on top of its holster. "But let me assure you that I work for some very impressive people too. And while I have no doubt a full-scale strike force of your fellow super-soldiers would be quite impressive, I am not so certain your Council would be willing to displace my company's rightful presence here on Acreon simply because you say so. I may be wrong. But who can say how these things would turn out?"

Neither man said anything for a moment but simply stared at one another. From the corner of his eye Roca was aware none of the other Drakenhof staff were moving either, all of them apparently transfixed by the confrontation taking place before them. Roca took the chance to re-evaluate the Drakenhof commandant.

He had dealt with uncooperative corporate representatives before, of course, even faced outright hostility from more than one provincial military commander. But there was something different about Patrin. Perhaps he had more strength than it had seemed at first.

The Commandant was certainly right about a few things. Roca knew he could, if he needed to, kill Patrin before he could take another breath. The dozen or so Drakenhof staff in the bunker would be no obstacle to him, particular with Mouse and Staker at his back, and he fancied their chances against even the hundreds of marines outside. And he could call in a Strike Team of Enforcers to blockade Acreon if he wanted to. But bulldozing a path across the galaxy was not his way.

The marine corporal, King, was shifting uncomfortably beside him and Roca could tell, again without looking, that both Mouse and Staker were ready to follow his lead if he chose violence. It was Corrick who broke the silence though.

"Sirs, please." he said," stepping slightly forwards as if to put himself between the Enforcer and the Commandant.

"There is really no need for this to go any further. Perhaps we did not state our – intentions clearly enough just now."

"Go on." said Roca, his hand still resting on his holster. Patrin did not move either.

"I believe," Corrick said, "what the commandant means to say is that you are all, of course, entitled to be here. Just as we are. That said, it would be tactically unsound, not to mention potentially dangerous if your mission, whatever it is, interfered with ours. Neither of us wants any friendly fire incidents and so on. It cannot help either of us to not know where the other one is. Wouldn't you agree?"

Roca conceded the point.

"So, to that end," Corrick said, "If you agree, Commandant, I believe I have a proposal that may serve both our purposes on Acreon."

It was a few hours since the meeting with the marine commandant, but she found him not in his barracks but in the base's medical centre, across the ATC tower from the command bunker. He was not in the main surgical wing or treatment rooms where most of the others who had survived Almar Square were being taken care of. Instead he was in the centre's small morgue unit.

It was warmer in there than she had expected it to be, barely any cooler than the outside climate. But all the dead of Drakenhof's campaign on Acreon were stored there in their caskets anyway, waiting for return en-masse to the company's homeworld.

The caskets, really little more than a rigid plastic backing over which a self-adjusting and self-sealing semi-transparent liner had been attached, would keep the remains of the dead sterile and presentable for as long as it took for their final journey back to Karkorum to be scheduled. Once received back at the company's headquarters, the tattoos of each corpse would be scanned and only then would the names of the dead be recorded as official losses in the company's books. Their final memorial would be a line in red ink in a Drakenhof ledger.

Any bodies not on a full-bond contract would be released to whatever family they had, along with any pay still owing after the deduction of expenses for packaging and shipping. The rest would be turned over to local recycling companies.

Until then, they were available for their fellow marines to pay their last respects.

King stood between the wheeled trolleys bearing the bodies of Sergeant Thole and his former partner, Stiller. Behind him lay the body of Ammit and, on another trolley, Niles. The medbots had been unable to save her from bleeding out and she had instead become another casualty of Almar Square. King was still wearing the bloody armour he had had on since the battle. His helmet sat on a table near the door to the room and his grenade launcher leaned up against it.

He looked old to her. Tired, almost broken. She guessed he could only be somewhere in his thirties and she wondered how many years of service he had put in. She wondered whether she would ever have looked like that if she hadn't joined the program.

He was a soldier though and she respected that, and the dead, so she coughed quietly to draw his attention.

He turned and looked up at her. She was standing just inside the doorway to the room, leaning back against the wall.

"Hey." he said. "You must be Mouse."

She nodded. "That I am. You got the word then?"

"I did." He tapped the comm-link on his chest as he turned back to the corpses. "I did. These things work great as long as you're less than twenty metres from the transmitter. Can't say I like it though."

"What's to like?" she said. "But we do what we gotta. For what it's worth, I don't think either of our bosses like it too much either."

King snorted a little. "Well, if Patrin okayed it, he must have a reason. That man never does anything unless he's getting something from it. What about your lieutenant? 'Roca', is it?"

"That's right." Mouse nodded.

"He's going along with it?"

"Yeah. I guess so. I guess he figures it's more trouble than it's worth to fight it. For now anyway."

King tapped the casket containing the remains of Stiller.

"He's got a funny way with words, your lieutenant." he said.

"What? 'Company Liaison'? Nah, I'm pretty sure calling you that was your man's idea."

King turned to face the Pathfinder and she could see now the redness around his eyes.

"No, not that." he said. "I mean the thing about killing that Veer-myn back in the city. The, er-"

"The Progenitor?"

King pointed at her in confirmation.

"Yeah, the Progenitor. Your man, 'Roca'. He said me and my team 'assisted' in killing it. It's a funny choice of words."

Mouse stayed silent, but she was beginning to suspect she knew what was coming next.

"I mean, the way he told it, it was as if you guys just

happened to be in the area, right? Like, you heard the sound of fighting and you rode in to the rescue, right?"

There was no sense of accusation in King's voice, no sound of anger. It was as if he was just stating a fact. But there was a coldness to his tone, an attitude in the way he stood that Mouse recognised. She felt the itch at the back of her skull she usually associated with an imminent fight.

"But I'm wondering if that's really how it played out." King said.

He looked around himself, at each of the four caskets awaiting cold-storage and shipment back to Karkorum. Niles, Stiller, Thole, and Ammit. All of them dead and silent.

"It just seems like a big coincidence that in the whole of Guiders City, you all just happened to be in the right place at the right time."

"That thing had to die. And it did. That's all that matters." Mouse said, wanting to end the conversation right there and then.

"Yeah, I don't doubt that." King said. "I'm just wondering if all these people really had to as well."

Mouse said nothing. She simply met his stare with her own as if she were daring him to say more. But he did not.

After a moment he turned away again.

"We're wheels up in five hours." Mouse said. "Be at the ship or we go without you, liaison or not. Oh, and one more thing."

"What?" King said.

"You capable of firing a weapon other than that grenade launcher?" Mouse said.

King turned towards his weapon and then looked at Mouse suspiciously.

"Yeah. Why?"

"Because where we're going, you're definitely going to want something a little lighter."

The Pathfinder turned to leave again but then she stopped, one hand resting on the frame of the doorway between the morgue and the treatment rooms.

"I'm sorry about your friends." she said. "I really am. But what's done is done. The mission is what matters."

Then she was gone.

King looked down at the ruined body of Ammit, his face pale and shiny beneath the layer of protective plastic.

"Yeah." said King. "That's what I thought you'd say."

CHAPTER 8

Dr Everret Markham flipped through the pages of a heavy, paper notebook, her long fingers turning the pages over quickly. The notebook was a reproduction, a copy of the writings of another scientist that had been confiscated by corporate security personnel some years previously. Its spine was thick and the pages were good quality synthetic stock, but already some were coming loose from their bindings and becoming dog-eared.

Within the book, hastily drawn diagrams and rough sketches of apparatus and ideas were mixed with the minutes of meetings and various schedules of operations. Everything was well ordered and presented, and the most pertinent parts and the insights most important to the author were underlined or circled in green. Just as Markham had once taught its author to do so. Over the green marks, Markham had made her own annotations using a red marker.

She came to the end of the notebook and closed it with a snap. She was starting to feel that she may have exhausted it of all its useful material.

She was in her laboratory, her own personal space.

Through its translucent walls she could some of the dozen other labs in the complex, all of which were technically 'hers' and all of which were equipped and run to her specifications, her schedule. But she still thought of this particular room as being hers alone and the workers in the rooms around her knew and respected that. They tended to leave her alone when she was in it.

Workbenches lined the room and a large heavy table dominated its centre. Glass jars full of reagents and electrical equipment covered much of the bench-space and beneath them were several metal storage cabinets. A large monitor was mounted on the wall at one end of the room and beneath it were the latest tissue samples she had received. There were three of them, each one a large level-4 containment jar with a bio-stasis field to keep its contents inert. To open them she had to have them taken to one of the more secure labs in the facility, but as they were, sealed tightly, they were safe enough. She knew even having them in her lab made some of her colleagues nervous, but she was the boss. She could do as she liked.

Opposite the samples, next to the room's only door, was a set of shelves and Markham had to stand on tiptoes slightly as she replaced the notebook in its space on the topmost shelf. 'Simmonds', was the name on the spine of the book she had just replaced. Next to it now were the reproduced works of several other scientists whose fate had been similar to that of Markham's former protégée. All of them had been brilliant in their own ways, but they had also all asked the wrong questions of the wrong people.

Markham stepped back, her hands on her hips, as she thought through what she had read and what she had to do next.

She turned back to the big table in the centre of the room and picked up her own electronic notebook. She pulled up the data her latest test had generated. The work was at a turning point, she could feel it. She and her small team of scientists were on the cusp of producing something truly magnificent. Something that would change the galaxy. She also knew, that if the next level of testing really did turn out as well as she thought it might, she would receive little, if any credit for it. At least not from anyone outside her small subterranean kingdom.

Her thoughts were interrupted as the lights in her laboratory darkened without warning and the clear walls of the room instantly became opaque. She felt the room's security measures go active. A sensor-dampening field sent a rippling sensation across her face and hands, the only parts of her body that were exposed. Then there was a brief metallic hum as an energy field winked into life across the doorway. The room had been isolated, physically and electronically, safety measures to prevent any other soul on the planet from seeing or hearing what happened within. The monitor set into the wall behind her connected to the secure communications network between her lab and the mainland.

A man's face appeared on the screen but she did not bother to either look up or to greet him. She simply flicked back through the pages of her notebook and resumed checking she had properly optimised the timings of her procedures for the next round of tests.

"Dr. Markham," said the face on the screen, apparently unbothered by her indifference. "How are we today?"

His face was obscured by a digital mask and his voice was modified, scrambled and recombined into a machine-like cant. Even if she met him in the flesh and they shared life stories, she doubted she would recognise him. But that was par for the course with these people. Ever since she had accepted the invitation from 'Dr Wolff' and left her safe and comfortable job in the Core, everything and everyone had been shrouded in secrecy. Except for herself, of course. They all knew who she was.

"'We' are fine," she said wearily, "and we are very busy." The schedule she had set for the work over the previous weeks had been more intense than she would have liked, but speed was an important part of the work. She could feel an ache starting to build in her forehead.

"I'm pleased to hear it," the face said, ignoring her tone. "So how goes the work? Have you had any more success?" Markham tried to relax her face as she moved past the screen and the tissue samples, still not looking up. There was a large incubator unit with a clear glass door on the workbench built into one side of the room and she bent over slightly to inspect it. The incubator's interior glowed with a soft, warm red light that gave the rack of five small plastic flasks an almost comforting, pleasant hue. But it was a misleading image. She knew the contents of any one of those flasks would kill her or any other human being in moments. But as they were, safely labelled and sealed, and stored in her lab, they seemed quite harmless.

"Yes and no." She walked back around her table and now she did face the monitor. She leaned back on the cold edge of the table behind her. "I added a new fold to the pseudo-protein membrane this week and successfully achieved encapsulation of the target pathogen. The simulations suggest this new structure has enhanced the contagious properties of the base molecule by a factor of at least six."

The face nodded appreciatively.

"So what's the catch?"

Markham sighed.

"Well, it is still likely to kill something like eighty percent of all life forms it infects."

The man on the screen shrugged and waved a hand as if this were a trifling detail.

"But secondly," Markham went on, "as you know, this is an extraordinarily resilient molecule. It has a very powerful, built-in mechanism that works very hard to bring it back to its original form. My capsule is still simply not stable enough. Not by a long way."

"I read your latest data," it said. "This one lasted much longer than the last one."

"Yes, there is that." Markham agreed. "And I think I know why. Whoever made this, this 'thing', I'm starting to understand them now. Whoever they are, or were, they were very, very clever."

"As clever as you?" the face said.

Markham arched an eyebrow towards the screen, refusing to be baited.

"Its mutagenic capacity alone is quite astounding. But I am working on a new modification now, one I think will extend the effective lifespan of the pseudo-protein capsule even further. I think, maybe even make it permanent this time."

The face on the screen sounded pleased.

"Very good." it said. "You may want to wait on that modification though."

"Oh? Why?" Markham was surprised. Since she had begun work on the project it had been clear that her new employers valued speed over nearly all other considerations.

"They're here. We have made contact with Enforcers earlier this evening."

She put down the notepad and tried to sound strong, despite the very real pang of fear she felt in her gut.

"They're here? How many?"

"Don't worry," the face said. "It's only one. Well, a small team. Anyway I am quite sure they do not know anything about you or the project. In fact, I think we both know that if they did, the entire planet would have been surrounded by now and we would most likely be dead already. So relax."

Markham thought for a moment and decided he was probably right.

"Yes. But still –"

"I know. Where there is one, more may follow. But they are being handled. They are only here because of our rat problem. The agents of the Council are always sniffing about, looking for trouble."

Markham rubbed her temple with the heel of her palm. Her headache was only getting worse.

"Get rid of them."

"They are being handled." the face said.

"Get rid of them." she repeated, but more urgently. "They may not know what we are doing here, but if they think you aren't in control of the Veer-myn, they could still place us under containment protocols. And that would be almost as bad."

The face nodded.

"The irony of it. But as I said, they are being handled. We've very nearly finished off the last of the Veer-myn anyway and once that is done it will all be over. I expect they will move on then. But, just in case…"

He hesitated.

"Yes?"

"Just in case," he said, "I think it would be wise to increase security at your location."

Markham sighed. More knuckle-draggers was the last thing she wanted wandering around her lab. She looked over at the incubating flasks again. Perhaps not the last thing.

"Very well. But only until the Enforcers are gone."

"Agreed. I also think it would be wise to transport your latest batch of processed pathogen off-world. Just in case"

Markham bit her lip. The samples, her work, this they would move to safety. Not her or her team.

"I will instruct some of the men I am sending to collect them and take them to another site." the face said.

Markham composed herself. She turned round and picked up her notebook again.

"Very well. If that is all, please let me know if there are any more – developments." she said.

"I will. And the same to you."

The screen winked out, the image of her companion being replaced by the slowly rotating image of the project logo. The lights came back up and the walls of the laboratory became transparent once more. She felt the buzz of the electronic countermeasures disengaging.

Now she could see some of her staff members in the next room, still busy at their own jobs. If they had noticed the security features activating they did not show it. None of them even looked up, let alone ask her who she had been talking to. They at least were all smart enough to know it was better not to ask questions.

Now that the call was over, she realised how hot she felt. The material of her lab-suit was heavy and by design not made to breathe. She walked over to a wall control and turned up the air-conditioning three notches before going to stand under the ceiling vent. Nothing happened though, no blast of fresh cool air washed over her. If anything, the air coming from the vent smelled a little stale.

She looked up at it, trying to peer between the narrow plastic slats as if she could somehow see far enough past them to divine why her room was so uncomfortably warm.

She reached over to the intercom panel on the wall beside her.

"Parnassa, come and see me, please. I have a job for you."

CHAPTER 9

There were several pull-down seats in the passenger bay of the Enforcers' ship, facing each other across a central aisle. Hand rails were built into the ceiling panels and there were closed equipment lockers above the seats, each labelled and stencilled with symbols King didn't recognise. At one end of the bay was the loading ramp and at the other a short ladder that led up to an access hatch to the ship's cockpit.

The Enforcer that King had heard being called 'Staker' had secured him in one of the slightly over-sized seats before strapping himself into one on the other side of the compartment. His duties to his passenger fulfilled, he appeared to have then fallen asleep, in spite of the roar of the aircraft's engines as the Accuser lifted off from Acreon's surface.

Everything about the Enforcers seemed slightly larger than it ought to be, including the safety gear. Staker had needed to heavily adjust the strapping on King's seat to make it fit the marine, a man who had never thought of himself as being small in any way, and hold him securely. King felt like a small child again, sitting in a grownup chair for the first time. His feet only just reached the floor and while his arms reached the armrests they felt awkwardly stretched.

As the Accuser bucked and rolled its way up through the atmosphere, he examined Staker in his couch opposite him.

His broad shoulders and heavy features reminded King of a trip he and his parents had once made when he was young.

They had travelled to a world back in the Third Sphere, the place where his parents had been born, and visited its biggest DreadBall stadium. It was the home of the three-time system-championship-winning SteerCorp Assassins. Outside the playing area, the pedestrian walkways were filled with stalls selling official replica workout jerseys, used balls and practice gear, even autographed programs and lithographs of the stars of the team. But between the vendors stood several tall statues, cast-metal images of some of the team's greatest stars of the past. Local legends like Curly Frees and Shan Singh had been immortalised in bronze with plaques at their feet explaining their place in the history of the Assassins. If you pressed the buttons set into their bases, you could even watch holo-replays of each player's greatest rushes, their most famous strikes and slams.

The statues were supposed to be life-sized representations of the men and women they honoured, but to a twelve-year old boy they had seemed much larger than life. No one could really be that big, that powerful, he had thought. But meeting the Enforcers had caused him to question that belief.

He felt a familiar lurching sensation in his gut as the noise of the engines died away to a quiet hum. They had broken out of the planet's atmosphere and he felt it as the artificial gravity generators kicked in. It felt like momentarily free-falling, a fleeting sense of vertigo and light-headedness as the body's senses adjusted to the subtly different pull. He resisted the urge to shake his head, knowing that would only further upset his equilibrium. After a moment of discomfort, his body caught up with what his mind was trying to tell it and he unfastened the strapping over his chest.

He stood and let the straps fall back onto his chair. The seat softly folded back up until it was almost flush with the bulkhead. Staker, still strapped in opposite him, did not move or open his eyes so King walked quietly up the gangway towards the cockpit. He had been ordered to accompany the Enforcers and so he had no choice in the matter. But if he was going to be Patrin's 'military liaison' he figured he might as well make the most of the experience. He knew he was in a position to see things no grunt marine ever did.

The access hatch cover swung upwards into a recess in the hull and he climbed forward and through it. The ship's cockpit was built for two, with seating for the pilot and systems operator set one behind the other. But it was also designed for heavily armoured and oversized Enforcers and King found there was enough spare room in it for him to crouch beside the rear seat.

There was a wide-field viewport built into the ship's forward bulkhead but King couldn't tell whether he was looking at a projection or through actual glass. Mouse was in the rear pilot's seat wearing a visored helmet that hid most of her face and she looked over her shoulder at King as he leaned forward, narrowing his eyes.

"Everything ok?" she said.

"Yeah," he replied. "Yeah, sure." Then, "Do you want me to leave?"

"No, it's fine. Just don't touch anything."

The starfield outside the viewport rolled as Mouse input-ted a course correction to the ship's engines. When it settled again the curve of Acreon's horizon lay beneath them. Above it lay the long shard-like shape of a starship.

"Is that the Genoa?" King said.

"It is," Mouse said as she checked a readout on a panel beside her seat. "She's powering up her local thrusters. Should be out of our way any moment now."

It was a striking sight and one King had never experi-enced before.

During his time in Drakenhof and the outfits he had worked for before them, King had been aboard perhaps a dozen interplanetary vessels. He had travelled light years, going from one star system to another to fight on one more worlds than he cared to remember. But in all those jour-neys he had never actually looked outside any of the ships upon which he had been transported.

Officer-class travel was probably different. But for long-hauls, all the grunt soldiers usually saw was the gang-way down to the cryogenics decks followed by the inside of a pod. Then they would be 'flash-frozen' – the slang name given to the process of rapid chemically-aided cool-ing that would put them in suspended animation for the journey – and see only the reverse of that route when they arrived at their destination. On shorter trips and intra-system point-to-point slides the passenger compart-ments were always windowless dormitories, anonymous spaces that looked pretty much the same from one ship to another. The defining characteristic of most, the meas-ure of quality by which marines often graded these things, was whether or not the bunks were double or triple stacked and how hard their mattresses were. Some ships, the better ones, had video screens you could access in the dorms that might include feeds relayed from the ship's collision detection cameras. But the view was limited and usually a grainy monochrome. You could get a better view of stars by punching yourself in the head.

Seeing outside the Accuser and seeing the Drakenhof strike cruiser anchored in orbit above Acreon was a novel luxury.

She stretched out across the Accuser's path, gleaming against the blackness of space. As they flew nearer King could make out the drive section and the bulging structures on the ship's side that housed its launch bays and weapons depots. Its main weapon, a huge plasma cannon built into its upper surface, was retracted and lay flat against its hull. Its other, smaller, ship-to-ship weapons were all hidden away behind sealed firing ports as the ship made ready to move off. The force on Acreon was due a resupply but King knew the ship would also be carrying the bodies of the company's dead back to Karkorum.

A light flashed on the instrument panel in front of Mouse. "There she goes." the Pathfinder said.

The engine array at the Genoa's stern flared into life and the ship began to silently move forward, gathering speed as she moved towards Acreon's slide point.

The Genoa would make most of her journey using its McKinley drive to create an artificial gravity-slope the ship could then 'slide' along, allowing it to cover great distances at faster than light speed. As efficient as the process was though, it was dangerous to engage the McKinley drive too close to a mass as large as a planet

She would first need to move at subluminal speeds to a point far enough away from Acreon that her slide drive would not be affected by the planet's gravity. Once there, she could accelerate away, using the NaviCorp to guide her path back to Karkorum.

King waved a quiet salute as he watched her go.

As the Genoa silently glided away, the distant lights of another ship orbiting the planet were revealed behind it.

"There's what we came for." said Mouse. "The CSS Hilton SP."

"Ok," said Roca from his seat in front of Mouse's. "She's nearly completed a full orbit so we're not far away from her. Mouse, bring us around her stern, please. I want to do a sweep of the hull before we go in."

The view outside the Accuser span again as Mouse put the Accuser into a roll and then pulled back on her stick to bring their path in line with their target. As they flew closer the distant light grew until it resolved into the outline of a starship.

The CSS Hilton SP was an early Stellargo-pattern hauler, long and thin, with a three hundred metre-long central trunk tipped at one end by a bridge section and at the other by an array of large thrusters. At 50,000 DWT, she was not a large ship. But she didn't need to be. She was not designed for truly long-distance hauls, nor did she require a large crew to maintain her. Just enough to set her course, secure her load, and make sure her local engines and McKinley drive were all functional.

In normal operation up to a dozen cargo pods could be mounted around her central axis, making her resemble a loaded revolver like the kind King had seen some Drakenhof officers wear on ceremonial duties. But stripped bare as she was when Roca's Accuser made its approach, her umbilical harness empty of the containers that were now on Acreon's surface, the Hilton resembled something more like the skeleton of a giant fish.

Mouse took the Accuser on a course that ran alongside the Hilton. The running lights along the hauler's spine were lit, as were those set into the angular surfaces of the command pod at her bow, but it was clear her viewports were all dark.

"A ghost ship." King said.

"Yeah?" said Mouse. "Well someone had to fly her here."

"There's a docking port." said Roca, pointing towards an area about halfway along the Hilton's length as they passed by it. "Mouse, can you put us on top of it?"

"Affirmative," the Pathfinder responded. "Bringing us back around."

The view outside the ship dipped and rolled as Mouse banked the Accuser and reversed its course.

Roca undid his harness and climbed out of his seat. Even with the exaggerated proportions built into the cockpit he had to half-roll out of it and stoop as he made his way towards King.

"Corporal King. I wonder if you have any experience with boarding actions?" he said.

King shook his head slowly. "No, not really. But don't worry, I won't get in your way, if that's what you're thinking."

"No, not at all." said Roca. "I'm sure you're a competent soldier. If you weren't I wouldn't have gone along with your commandant attaching you to my team. But all the same, you are part of my command now and I'll expect you to follow my orders. Is that going to be a problem?"

King swallowed back his pride.

"No," he said. "Not at all. If they tell me to go with you, I go with you."

Roca seemed satisfied with that.

"Good. Once we're aboard the ship, keep up and stay behind us."

A dull clang sounded from beneath them and the ship shuddered slightly as the Accuser's docking port connected with the Hilton's. Mouse released the flight controls as she began to power down the Enforcer ship.

"So no one from your outfit's been aboard the Hilton since it got here?" she said.

"No," King said as he turned and began to climb back down into the passenger compartment. "Not part of the contract. Our tasking was to eliminate the Veer-myn invaders, that's all. Doesn't really matter where they came from, does it?"

"The mission is all that matters?" said Mouse. King ignored the barb.

"Yeah, something like that." he said. "So, what do you think we'll find in there, Lieutenant?"

Roca was right behind him and he looked back over his shoulder at the silent drifting ship.

"Hopefully some answers. Where she came from, how she got here. Maybe even her crew. But at least we won't have to cut our way into this one. Corporal King, would you wake Staker and tell him to start cycling the docking lock, please?"

The port opened onto the main deck of the Hilton.

The readout on the Accuser-side of the docking port had reported breathable atmosphere within the hauler. The Enforcers had all donned full helmets though and King had attached a borrowed breathing mask borrowed from one of the equipment lockers to his.

It was dark when they climbed down the extendable

ladder from the belly of the Accuser. The main overhead strip lights were all off and the only light came from lines of red auxiliary LEDs running along both sides of the deck. Each of the four boarding party members switched on the lights on their helmets and weapons and flashed them up and down the long gangway. Nothing moved though – no alien raiders or stranded crewmen were there to greet them.

Once the port was closed and re-sealed to protect the Accuser, Roca flipped open the cover on his wrist-unit and confirmed the environmental check with his armour's own sensors.

"Pressure looks good, gas levels all fine. A little high on the CO_2, but tolerable. Even for you." Roca nodded in King's direction. "Cold though."

The Forward Observer's faceplate retracted into his helmet and King undid the straps on his mask.

King didn't need the expert opinion of a Forward Observer to tell him it was cold on the ship. Under his armourweave plates he was wearing a uniform designed for the surface heat of Acreon in summer and he was wishing he had taken the time to layer on some warmer undergarments before boarding the Accuser. In the beams of the party's torches he could see his exhaled breath condensing in the frigid air like fleeting ghosts.

He was not prepared for the smell either. It was like a mix of curdled milk and rotten garbage.

"What is that?" he said, his nose wrinkling as he sniffed the air.

The Enforcers looked at each other in the dim light of the corridor.

"Nothing good." said Roca.

"Atmosphere and grav though." Mouse said, taking a

few soft testing steps. "Suggests someone's still alive here somewhere."

Roca flicked the light built into the side of his helmet up and over the cantilevered frame of the Hilton's interior. "Yes, Could be. But these old ships are built for maximum automation. Most of their systems are set to run more or less forever."

"So, what's the plan, Lieutenant?" asked Staker. He had removed his helmet and clipped it to his belt and his eyes glittered in the darkness. He was clearly keen to be on the move again.

Roca closed the cover on his wrist unit and looked both ways along the passage, his headlight fading into the darkness in either direction.

"I looked up the schematics for this class of ship on the way up here. Most of its internal structure is on this single level but there should be access to the crew deck up near the bridge. Mouse and King, you're with me. We'll go forward, see if anyone's home up there. Staker, you'll go aft. Check out the drive section. See what you can find."

Staker nodded his understanding and turned towards the ship's stern.

"Staker."

"Yeah, Mouse?"

"Be careful back there. We don't know what happened to this ship, keep your eyes open."

"Yeah, understood." Staker rotated the end of the torch on his rifle, extinguishing its light. Then, rifle cradled in his arms, he walked away from them and into the darkness.

Roca turned the towards the ship's bow. "Mouse, lead the way."

The two Enforcers silently moved out but King paused

for a moment and checked the primer on the rifle he had brought with him. It was the same one he had taken from Stiller's body and it was fully loaded. He switched its activator to automatic before following them towards the bridge.

The Hilton was not the first ghost mission King had ever been on.

Frontier life, life on worlds in the Fourth and Fifth expansion Spheres of the GCPS, even on a relatively well-developed Fourth Sphere world like Acreon was hard, harder than people in the settled and prosperous worlds of the Core and the inner spheres might believe. The failure rate for colony worlds and pioneer outposts was high.

When a world was marked for settlement or exploitation it would usually receive an allotment of Shensig containers, all filled with the basic supplies calculated to be sufficient to get whatever endeavour was planned started. But after that, the colonists were then often on their own.

Unless the leaseholder on an outer sphere world had deep pockets, or a particularly precious resource had been located, military support or evac ships might be weeks or months away. King himself had been on several missions to save, salvage, or simply mop up what was left of a frontier outpost that had fallen foul of local conditions.

Sometimes rescue teams would arrive to find a colony that had been wiped out by a novel disease. Other times extremes of weather or establishing supplies of food and water had been the problem. Hostile aliens were also a common threat, but, on occasion, what had killed off a colony was less clear.

King had worked a job once with a small private security consultant, answering an automated distress beacon calling from a metal-working station on the third moon orbiting the Cleos gas giant. He had been a rookie back then, taking one of his first contracts since leaving Acreon. Whatever had happened on Cleos III, it was all over by the time he and his men arrived on the scene. They had found the beacon, still working, still sounding its call from the office of the station's head administrator, but it was at the centre of a ghost town, entirely empty of life. Most unnervingly, there had been no signs of violent struggle. The client company's full complement of vehicles was still in its streets and all the mining equipment and installations were also present and apparently operational. Only the people had vanished, leaving behind empty, echoing homes and silent offices, but no clue as to where or why or how they had gone.

The Hilton was beginning to feel like Cleos III had.

They had neither seen nor heard any sign of life on the way along the main deck but there was no sign of any fighting – no blood trails or burn marks – to be found either. Now King, Roca, and Mouse were gathered around the hatch in the decking that led to the crew compartments on the lower deck. It was magnetically sealed.

"Failsafe device?" King said. Mouse nodded.

"Yeah, seals automatically to protect the crew down there. Keeps them and their atmosphere sealed up nice and safe. But it's a failsafe for a hull breach and," Mouse looked around the darkened corridor, "there's no breach."

"No override?" said Roca.

Mouse shrugged and stood up. "No. Once the failsafe is triggered it's designed not to be opened from the outside."

She patted a pouch on her hip. "I've got the tools, so in theory I could break it. But there's no power. I'm guessing we'd need to reroute something from the bridge to do it."

"The bridge it is then." Roca said.

The double-width door to the bridge should have slid open automatically when they approached it but instead it had to be forced open. King and Mouse each took a side and pulled the two doors apart while Roca knelt a few metres away from them, his rifle aimed at whatever lay beyond the portal.

But the bridge was empty.

Five empty crew stations were positioned around the room, each one set in front of blank, silent screens and projectors that ought to have been alive with readouts from the ship's various systems.

The only sign anyone had been there before them was a single wall panel that lay on the floor of the room, exposing bundles of wires and circuit panels on the inside of the bridge's bulkheads.

While Roca and King watched her back, Mouse knelt down and, after a quick examination, declared the circuits that powered many of the basic systems, including the lighting in most of the main corridor and the doors to the bridge and crew areas, had been cut.

"But why would anyone do that?" King asked. "And where did they go after they did it?"

"I don't know," said Roca, "But I think we need to find out. Mouse, can you get the power back on up here?"

Mouse considered the exposed innards of the ship.

"Yeah, I think so. Maybe not the whole ship, but I can get the bridge systems back up at least."

"Good," said Roca. "See if you can get the crew hatch open too."

***

Staker moved silently but quickly towards the stern of the Hilton, slipping easily through the shadows. He had, as ordered, kept his eyes open the whole way, but there had been absolutely nothing to see the in ship's central corridor. Still, he had a growing suspicion that he might not be entirely alone in the ship's rear section.

Over his years of service as an Enforcer, he had developed something of a sense for danger and he felt it nagging at the back of his mind as he reached the stern access panels to the ship's umbilical frame.

On a Stellargo-pattern hauler, there was only limited access from the ship's interior to its cargo pods. The whole point of the design was that cargo could be attached and removed quickly and easily, allowing the ship to spend the minimum amount of time in orbit or at a docking station. Time spent standing still was time not spent earning credits. But ships like the Hilton were still subject to the occasional customs inspections or found their pods in need of small repairs along their journeys. For this reason, a small but functional airlock was built into the side of the Hilton.

It led to a vac-sealed crawl-way, part of the umbilical harness that ran around the cargo hauler, and Staker stopped at its access hatch. The hatch appeared to have been forced open.

He could see its locking mechanism was bent and buckled in towards the ship, as if someone or something had applied a great deal of pressure to get in from the other side.

The interior of the crawl-way was too dark even for Staker's enhanced eyesight to see much, but it was not the only sense the Enforcer program had improved. He sniffed the air and recognised the smell of hydraulic fluids, the kind that would be used to operate the release mechanisms. He decided to risk a flash of light from the torch affixed to his rifle and shone it into the crawl-way. Spots of dark and oily fluid glistened in the beam. On their far side he could see the sealed outer hatch.

He was about to contact Roca and tell him what he had found when a noise from his right, towards the stern of the ship, caused him to spin round, his rifle snapping up to his shoulder as he stepped smoothly into a firing stance. But he could see nothing, only the door to the main engine section, a faded corporate logo stencilled across its heavy metal surface.

He was sure he had heard something though – a faint metallic rattling – and he held his position for a moment, waiting for it to repeat. When it did not, he sniffed the air, but smelled only the oil from the crawl-way again.

He switched off his weapon's light and moved cautiously towards the engine room door.

It was not locked and Staker slowly pulled it open, taking care to do so as quietly as possible.

Beyond it was a combination machine room and workshop, filled with racks of tools and cabinets covered in scuffed and worn paint. A solid-looking workbench filled up most of the centre of the room and it was laden with more tools and spare parts. A welding kit that looked like it was in the middle of being broken down for repair lay at the far end, and behind the table was another closed hatch. A metal sign bolted above it read; 'Danger: Engine Room'

He could smell something different in the air now, something more bitter and biological than the odours of engine oil and cleaning fluids. It was the sweet, funky smell again, but stronger. Fresher.

He glanced back behind himself before moving to the

right of the workbench and through the machine room.

The machine room was much warmer than the rest of the ship had been and as he got closer to the hatch at its far end Staker could hear the soft rumbling of the Hilton's reaction chambers on the other side. He was not surprised by this. Ships often kept their local engines on at a low power setting, even between journeys, as it was generally more economical than to repeatedly shut down and restart them. But he still took great care opening the door.

Power for the engines was generated within two huge cylindrical stacks that ran lengthwise away from Staker for nearly twenty metres. They would split again further on, either in the next compartment or possibly on an external engine mounting, and even idling, the heat they generated was enough to make a light sweat start to bead on Staker's shaven head. Staker froze in place though, his finger resting on the trigger of his weapon, when he saw the carpet of Veer-myn bodies laid out beneath the engine stacks.

The floor was thick with them. There were at least forty Nightcrawlers, their thin bodies curled around one another, their long limbs draped languidly over their neighbours, and at first Staker thought they might be dead. But as he stood and observed them he noticed the occasional movement – a twitching snout, a slowly curling tail – and he realised the Veer-myn were in fact dozing. They were basking in the warmth of the engine stacks, seeking, Staker assumed, refuge from the cold that filled the rest of the ship.

Somehow, for some reason, these Veer-myn had broken out of the cargo pod they had been contained in and then must have used the hatch to access the ship itself. Had they done that before or after the ship had arrived at Acreon though? He didn't know, but it wasn't his mission to work these things out, only to report what he had found. He began to back out of the engine room.

The loud hum of the stacks' internal reactions had drowned out any sound his entrance had made. As he began to slowly back out of the engine room though an alarm tone suddenly filled the engine room and an orange emergency light set into the bulkhead above him began to rotate and flash. The quiet rumbling of the engine stacks was replaced by a building, whining noise, growing in intensity as the reactions within them sped up.

Staker felt the artificial gravity in the deck beneath his feet fluctuate, lessening in strength for just a second before the ship seemed to jerk forwards roughly, shaking him and everything else in the maintenance room and engine compartment. Some of the tools in the machine room behind him fell from their racks, crashing noisily to the metal deck.

He froze again and, for a moment, thought he might yet get away with it. But then one of the Veer-myn beneath the stack to his left slowly raised its elongated animal head. It sniffed repeatedly at the air and its snout turned towards Staker, still standing in the doorway out of the engine room. The Nightcrawler's eyes widened as it saw the human intruder and realised what he was. It opened its mouth to hiss and alert its mates but Staker shot it through the skull before it could make a sound.

CHAPTER 10

"What in the Core was that?"

The lights in the bridge had all come on and the displays and screens around the crew stations were flooding the room with shining colours. But what had King worried was the sudden jump forward they had all felt.

Mouse was up to her armpits in the exposed bulkhead and she wiggled free before running over to one of the control positions. She stabbed at the buttons set into the panel on the seat's armrest, quickly digesting what the screens in front of it were showing her. She frowned darkly.

"That," she said, "was the main engines engaging. We are now moving."

"We're moving? But why?" King said.

Mouse looked back over her shoulder towards the electronic bypass device she had just installed into the bridge's circuitry.

"We did this, Sergeant?" said Roca. He stood at the entrance to the room, where he had been guarding the still-open doors.

Mouse had sat down on the edge of the chair now and she

pulled up a series of diagnostic interfaces until she found one that showed her data being read directly from the ship's engines.

"I think so. It's hard to tell. I mean, I didn't do anything to the drives, just rebooted the local power, but – "

"But the engines came on anyway." said Roca.

"Yeah," Mouse said. "The ship's computer is telling me they were always 'on', they were just at a low power output. But something sent them into overdrive and now we're –" She paused as Roca leaned in behind her. "What the hell?"

King tried to read the screen over Mouse's other shoulder but it made no sense to him. If it had been a schematic for a weapon or a military deployment diagram he might have been in his element, but the scrolling numbers and alphanumeric codes he saw flashing by were far beyond his training.

"What's happening?" he said. "What's does it all mean?"

"It means we're moving along a pre-set course here. Something programmed into the NaviCorp. We're building up speed now, but the ship will take us there in about thirty minutes."

"Where?" said King, his mind racing. Being ordered to take a short trip into orbit with the Enforcers was one thing. He had not counted on making any interstellar journeys too. "Where's it taking us?"

Mouse looked up at him.

"Straight into Acreon. We're going to crash into Guiders City."

A wave of vertigo washed over King and he stepped away from the two Enforcers. He rubbed his hand against his forehead as he tried to make sense of what Mouse had told him.

He was no engineer, nor a great mathematician. He didn't

pretend to understand much of the science of warfare or even much of the technology he employed on a daily basis as a soldier. But he had learned enough about the basic concepts of mass and energy preservation to know what the impact of a piece of flaming metal the size of the Hilton could do to Guiders City. The Hilton's cargo pods had started fires that had destroyed much of the place. The Hilton itself would wipe the city off the surface of the planet.

"Mouse, can you stop it?" Roca said.

Mouse pulled up another screen, a circuitry diagram from the Hilton's own technical manual, and threw a sidelong glance towards the bypass device as if it, the very machine she had installed, had somehow betrayed her.

"Yeah, I think so. No promises though."

"Good enough. Get on it. I'll go down to the engine room, see if Staker and I can do anything from that end."

Roca took a step away from the Pathfinder's chair and keyed on his comm unit.

"Staker, this is Roca, do you copy?" He waited a moment but there was no answer.

"Staker, Roca, come in."

Again there was no immediate answer, and Mouse was halfway from her chair to the wall panel when a burst of static rang through all their comm links. Then they heard Staker's voice, garbled and broken as if his signal was suffering from some kind of electronic interference.

"-ontact! -epeat, -tact!"

Between Staker's urgent words they could hear the rapid staccato reports of gunfire and harsh, animal screeches.

Roca's faceplate snapped shut, sealing his armour as he unslung his rifle and ran back towards the open doors.

"Staker, Roca. I'm on my way."

Before he left the room he half-turned and shouted over his shoulder.

"Mouse, get that guidance system back online. Do whatever you have to. King, sweep the crew compartment. Both of you be ready to leave in a hurry if you need to."

Before King could say anything, Roca was gone.

Staker's rifle barked, flashes of hot gases lighting the confined space of the machinery bay. The weapon was a supreme piece of engineering, one of the finest Accutek had ever made, at least in Staker's opinion, and it was doing its job well aboard the Hilton.

The HPR-45 was one model in the class known generically as a Tag rifle, a hybrid weapon somewhere between a pup-sized automatic carbine and a longer-barrelled sniper weapon. As circumstances required, it could fire a variety of tracking rounds, low impact solid shots that could return several optional tracking signals – infrared, radio, even pheromonal depending on the nature of the target.

At Almar Square he had used it to fire a strobing infrared round to mark the Progenitor, something the Accuser's weapons systems had been able to lock onto quickly and easily, allowing the ship's Polaris cannons to destroy the Veer-myn beast with inescapable accuracy. Right now he was using it in its more basic but no less effective configuration as a close-quarters combat firearm. With a shortened barrel and stock it sacrificed some accuracy but that didn't matter in the confined space of the Hilton's compartments.

A Veer-myn leaped across the workbench towards him and Staker dropped it with a shot to the head. Its skull exploded from the exit wound and the body fell limply to the bench's surface. Another Nightcrawler immediately took its place though, and Staker fired again. This one seemed faster than its predecessor and it dodged to one side. Staker's first two shots missed his target completely and ricocheted noisily off the bulkhead behind it, but the third shot hit it squarely in the shoulder. The round tore off a bloody chunk of flesh in a spray of dark blood and sent the screeching Veer-myn spinning down to the deck.

There were others behind it, pushing in through the hatch from the engine room and snapping and hissing at Staker through mouths filled with sharp yellow teeth. They seemed somehow different to the Veer-myn he had observed on the planet below. They were leaner, thinner, and he guessed they must have run out of food on the drifting Hilton some time ago. Some were armed with knives, others seemed only to have their claws to fight with, but at least a few had ray-guns and they were firing back at him. Their shots were characteristically wild but he knew it was only a matter of time before one of them hit him. His chest and head were protected but he was starting to think his decision not wear full combat armour for the mission might have been a mistake.

He continued to back away through the machine room, firing at the Veer-myn every few steps. He was nearly all the way to the compartments' exit but he knew he had to balance haste with combat effectiveness. He had to get out quickly lest he be overwhelmed and torn apart by the horde of hungry Veer-myn he had discovered. But he also knew how fast a Veer-myn could move so simply turning and running was out of the question. If he could get out of the machine room and find a way to seal the hatch, he might be able to contain the alien horde, at least for a while.

Staker did not know the complete details of what had

been done to him when he had become an Enforcer. He could not remember much of the process or even much of his life before joining the program when it came down to it. But he knew the people that ran the corps had rebuilt his body, that they had stripped out the weakest parts of it and replaced them with superior, vat-grown and engineered tissues and organs. And he was happy to accept that these things had been done. Whatever the doctors and medical technicians had taken out of the man he had been when he stepped aboard the Enforcer recruitment vessel, they had given him back so much more.

He was faster and stronger than any unenhanced human – that much was a given. But his mind was immeasurably sharper than it ever could have been too.

They called it 'combat conditioning' – a state of mind that to Staker felt like entering a higher level of awareness. When it kicked in, as it had when the Veer-myn had surged towards him, it felt almost as if time itself slowed down and all considerations other than carrying out his mission, of killing, of surviving, of doing whatever it was the Council required of him in the moment, faded away into obscurity.

It was as if everything that existed between his mind and the finger that pulled the trigger of his weapon was gone. There was no fear, no anger, not even hatred. Just a cold-blooded drive to kill and kill and kill as fast and smoothly as he could without hesitation or regret or even any concern for his own well-being, insofar as it did not affect his combat-effectiveness. Free from all other concerns and feelings, his reaction times were almost instantaneous. His processing of the input his senses delivered to his brain stem was uncluttered and unfettered and resulted in imme-diate control impulses being sent to his muscles.

He fired four shots in the space of a second at four separate targets, all of them in motion and intent on killing him, all while he himself was also moving in the opposite direction. With one hand he flung a short knife from a sheath on his hip, impaling a Veer-myn warrior through its throat, leaving it clutching at its severed arteries as they sprayed bright blood between its clawed fingers. With the other he smoothly dropped the empty magazine from his rifle and slammed in a fresh one. He was a machine, free of emotion and possessed of one purpose – to fight, kill, and survive. He was less than two metres from the hatch back out into the ship's main deck now and nothing could stop him.

But his accelerated perception could also be a curse. It was what allowed him to see the shot he fired that was meant to decapitate a hideous Veer-myn warrior instead bounce off the metallic rim of the welder's goggles it was wearing over its snout. The impact knocked the Veer-myn over and Staker heard the crunch of its orbital bone breaking, but he also saw the flattened solid round he had fired travel at a simply unpredictable angle, towards the pressurised gas canister of the broken-down welder on the workbench next to it.

The explosion shredded the Veer-myn with the broken eye socket and threw its nearest mates into the bulkhead behind them. Staker threw himself to the deck, but even his enhanced reflexes could not stop the wave of shrapnel that engulfed him.

The metallic ring of his armoured boots echoed from the angled bulkheads all around him as Roca ran. Stealth was no longer of any concern now and he ran even faster when he heard a muffled explosion from somewhere up ahead.

He passed by the access hatch to the umbilical framework, the one Staker had noticed had been forced open, without pausing. A few metres beyond it was the entrance to the engine section, a faded corporate logo stencilled across the heavy-looking door. He could see and smell greasy smoke spilling out from beyond it but he could no longer hear any gunfire.

He slowed and slung his rifle and then drew his pistol from its holster at his hip. With his free hand he reached out towards the handle on the side of the hatch.

Smoke billowed out from the hatch as it opened towards him but the filters in his armour stopped him from choking and fed him clean air.

Within the compartment he could see tools and ship parts scattered across the floor and at the far end of a heavy workbench in the room's centre lay the source of the thick black clouds. Some kind of machine had exploded there and its burning remains and whatever fuel it had contained had started several other small fires, including one at the far corner of the compartment. The flames were licking at several tall canisters of what appeared to be some kind of compressed gas.

Movement in the shadows to his left caught his eye. He switched his helmet's visor to infrared and saw now there were two figures on the deck, one astride the other, glowing white in his heat-sensitive vision. His sensors identified the bottom of the two as Staker while the scrawny frame and the long tail that whipped frantically to and fro marked the other as a Veer-myn.

The bio-sensors in Roca's armour told him Staker was already dead. He could see a pool of dark blood around the Pathfinders shoulders and there were several jagged wounds on his arms and face. The rest of his body was obscured by the Veer-myn straddling him.

It was thin, thinner than even the scrawniest Nightcrawler he had ever seen before. Its muzzle was buried in Staker's body, between the Enforcer's head and his left shoulder, and Roca could hear small crunching noises coming from its mouth. The alien was starving and was trying to bite through the dead Enforcer's armour. So intent was it on trying to get at its meal, it seemed entirely oblivious of Roca's presence.

A wave of revulsion and anger surged up in Roca and he lifted the muzzle of his weapon, ready to blasting the ravenous Veer-myn apart. But before he could pull the trigger, his combat conditioning kicked in.

He felt his emotions drain away and be replaced by a much colder and more clinical state of mind. The abomination he was seeing was still there on the deck, his dead teammate too. But now he saw the Nightcrawler as simply a target to be eliminated and, as more bright shapes appeared in the doorway at the far end of the machine room, not the only one.

Staker had uncovered their nest, and his weapon's fire and the small explosion he seemed to have caused had held them at bay. But now they could smell blood and several more Veer-myn were moving hesitantly through the hatch.

Roca knew the Veer-myn had good low-light vision, but it seemed they could not see him through the smoke. He knew he could use that to his advantage.

The deck plating was beginning to vibrate and rattle beneath his feet as the Hilton started to break into Acreon's atmosphere, and Roca's eyes flickered towards the gas tanks he had noticed earlier. Keeping his weapon trained on the Veer-myn on top of Staker, he slowly removed a grenade from his belt with his other hand and rotated its detonation timer with his thumb.

It was time to leave the CSS Hilton SP.

"Ok. I'm going in now." King said.

He crouched down, one hand on his rifle's grip, the other on the handle built into the crew compartment hatch, and pulled. The hatch swung open with a pneumatic hiss and locked into position against the side of the corridor.

He aimed his rifle through the hatch, the light on the side of its barrel picking out a metal ladder and the deck below. He slung his rifle and began to climb down.

As he reached the bottom rungs, lights set into the ceiling around the room automatically activated, revealing a communal crew area.

One side of the compartment was almost entirely taken up by a pre-formed plastic dining area. A low round table was surrounded by a curved couch built into the bulkhead behind it and a few stools all bolted to the floor. Storage lockers and a pair of battered rehydration machines that looked as old as the ship itself filled the opposite wall and a small vidscreen had been fitted to a corner facing the dining area. It was bare, functional décor, and it was completely uninhabited.

There was almost no sign of life at all. The table was clear – no half-eaten meals, not even the bottles of water crew members might leave out ready for when they awoke after a long transit. Only the scratches on the table's surface and scuff marks on the deck around the lockers told King anyone had ever been there at all. He unslung his rifle anyway before moving into the next compartment.

He found the ship's flash-freeze pods, six of them in a line. But they were all empty too, their clear canopies raised expectantly above their white-padded beds, their monitor screens all dark.

The spectre of Cleos III rose in his mind once more.

As he made his way back through the dining area and up the ladder to the main deck, he could hear and feel the growing vibration building in the ship's frame. The decking and the ship's bulkheads were beginning to creak and rattle all around him and when he breathed out he realised he could no longer see his breath. The frigid ship was warming up as it entered Acreon's atmosphere.

He was closing the hatch again when he heard a massive explosion from the rear of the ship. He kneeled beside the hatch for a moment his hand still on its handle, staring into the gloomy stern of the Hilton.

"King, do you copy?" It was Mouse, speaking through his comm-link. He had to run up the volume on his unit to hear her over the sound of the ship's groaning super-structure.

"Yeah, barely. Finished my sweep. There was nobody down there. I just heard something from the back of the ship though. Sounded bad."

"Affirmative to that." the Enforcer said. "Roca has engaged. You need to get down there. Help him out."

King stood and turned towards the bridge of the ship. He was some way off now, but as he shone his helmet's torch it looked as if the doors at the entrance to the bridge were closed now.

"What? Why? What's going on? What did they find?" Numerous other questions were running through his mind, including what could possibly be aboard the Hilton that two Enforcers would need the help of a single marine to deal with. But Mouse did not give him time to answer them.

"Doesn't matter. There'll be time to swap exciting stories later. Right now, you need to get your ass to the docking port and meet up with the lieutenant. Do you copy, marine?"

It was the same tone of voice he had heard back in Almar Square – firm, commanding, a little disdainful. An Enforcer giving a command to a subordinate. But just like in the square, King knew he had no real choice.

"Ok," he said. "I'm on my way."

King was nearly at the docking port when he heard something large and heavy coming towards him from the ship's stern. Roca jogged out of the gloom, a grim look on his face.

"Corporal King," he said as he reached up for the retractable ladder that was built into the docking port above him. "Where's Mouse?"

"Mouse?" said King. "She's still on the bridge. Where's Staker?" He looked back along the gangway behind Roca but there was no sign of the other Enforcer.

Roca's faceplate retracted into his helmet as he entered the security codes into his wrist unit to unlock the port.

"Staker's gone." he said, ignoring the shocked look on King's face. "I bought us some time, but we need to leave immediately."

The locks in the docking port clicked and whirred above them as it opened. Roca turned towards the bridge.

"Sergeant Mouse, Roca, come in. Mouse, do you copy?"

"Copy, Roca, this is Mouse."

Her voice was slightly distorted and the noise from the ship's superstructure as it struggled through Acreon's atmosphere made it hard to hear. Roca tapped King on the shoulder and signalled him to start climbing up into the Accuser with a hand movement.

"Sergeant, I thought I told you to meet me at the docking port." he said.

"Affirmative, Roca, you did. But that was before I managed to get some control over the ship."

King paused, halfway up the ladder.

"How much control?" Roca said.

"I can steer it to some degree" Mouse said. "But I can't stop it. I'm locked out of a lot of the links between the bridge and the engines and every time I get control the system boots me out again."

"Can you get us back into orbit?" Roca asked.

"No. Not a chance. This thing is going down no matter what I do. I can't stop it from hitting the planet, but I can stop it from hitting its target."

"Its target?" King said. He had to shout to be heard now. "Does she mean Guiders?"

"Affirmative," Mouse said. "I wasn't sure, but I'm certain of it now. Roca, I think this whole thing was a trap."

"A trap?" Roca said.

"The crew compartment failsafe. There's some weird code in the ship's computer, definitely not standard corporate issue. But it was set to trigger as soon as anyone tried to access the crew compartment. Sir, this was no accident. This ship is programmed to destroy Guiders City."

Roca looked back towards the stern of the ship and he unshouldered his rifle. King followed his gaze. Was that movement he saw in the shadows at the edge of his vision?

"Understood," Roca said. "Can you rig something up? Some kind of fix that will –"

"Negative, Roca. This code is – it's really good. I don't have nearly enough time to unpick it all. As long as I'm up here I can keep stalling the system, stop it taking the ship into the landmass. Get it out over the ocean. She'll keep descending, but if I let go of the reins, this thing will go straight into the city."

Roca held his rifle up, sighting down into the stern of the ship. Dark shapes were moving along the gangway towards them.

"King, what's the population of Guiders?" he said.

King thought for a moment.

"Before the invasion, maybe fifty thousand. Less than half that now, but still…"

"Unacceptable." Roca said. "Mouse, can you minimise casualties?"

"Yes, sir." Mouse said. She'll keep descending, I can't turn the engines off. But I should be able to make sure she hits at sea. There's gonna be one hell of a splash, but she shouldn't hit anything manned. You all need to go now though. The turbulence is going to tear the Accuser off any minute. If you go now, it'll still be a rough ride and you're half the pilot I am, but you can still make it."

Roca lowered his rifle and moved towards the ladder.

"Understood." He took hold of the rung below King's feet and looked up expectantly. King was frozen, stunned by how quickly wanted to protest, to say something, anything. Even for Enforcers, Roca's apparent willingness to abandon his team mate seemed cold and harsh.

Before he could say anything though, his comm link chimed and he keyed it on. It was a closed channel between himself and Mouse.

"King," Mouse said over the comm-link. "One last thing.

I know you don't have much reason to trust us. But remember – we're not the bad guys."

"Separation in 5...4...3...2...1..."

Roca hit the switch to break the docking port seal and disengage the clamps that held the Accuser tight to the hull of the Hilton. As soon as he felt them release, he began to pull the stick back and his ship began to fight its way through the turbulence the Hilton was creating beneath it.

Separating the two ships while still in the vacuum of space would have been infinitely preferable to what he was trying to do now. The dangers inherent in trying to separate two objects in the fires of atmospheric re-entry while travelling at hundreds of kilometres per hour were immense. But he had no other choice.

Plumes of flame had been streaming from the bow of the Hilton and back towards and over the Accuser by the time he and King had buckled themselves into the two pilot's seats and Roca had powered up his ship for departure. The viewports were obscured as the hauler broke through Acreon's atmosphere and he had been entirely reliant on instruments and intuition to tell him exactly where they were. The coupled ships had shaken so violently he had considered it a very real possibility his mission was about to end in utter failure, that his ship and what was left of his team would simply be torn apart by the descent or dragged down to the surface with the Hilton.

Then the flames had cleared, most of them at least, and outside his ship he had seen glimpses of clear blue skies. The prow of the Hilton was still burning though, throwing up streamers of black smoke and small pieces of debris from her damaged hull, and he could only hope whatever had caught light during her passage out of the vacuum would not spread to his own ship. But it was time to get clear.

As the Accuser lifted away from the Hilton and he began to put her into a roll away to the right, Roca could hear more impacts on the bottom of his ship as small pieces of the Hilton struck her. The ship was still shaking as moved through the Hilton's wash.

Without warning, the Accuser suddenly lurched to one side, and King and Roca were both thrown hard against their restraints as the ship shook violently. Numerous alarms began sounding throughout the cockpit and Roca scanned the urgent warning messages being flashed onto the console in front of him.

"What was that?" King yelled from the seat behind him.

"We lost an engine." Roca shouted back. "Something big hit us."

As well as telling him his left engine was no longer functional, the ship's computer was also registering damage to the fuel line to the right engine and counselling the pilot to seek mechanical attention immediately. He switched it off.

Alarm signals were still flashing on several other screens though and the ship was losing height quickly.

He pulled up the NaviCorp screen. They had made re-entry some distance from the coast of Guiders City and his mind raced as he calculated the ship's fall rate. He scowled when he realised the ship would hit the water at least four kilometres short of land.

Time was running out for the Accuser. He flipped on the forward-facing radar scanner, setting it to search for somewhere, anywhere, he could put his ship down safely.

Hold tight," he called to King. "Looks like we're going in."

He was interrupted by an urgent beeping from the

forward-scanning radar and he quickly scanned the display.

"Wait," he said. "There's land not far from here. Looks like a small island. We should be able to at least get close to it."

He hauled the stick over to his left, struggling with the twin forces of impetus and gravity to adjust the Accuser's headlong course, while in his head he began to adjust his numbers, trying to calculate again whether the ship had enough altitude, enough time to reach dry land.

In his own seat, King stabbed a finger at the unfamiliar screen set into the panel before him until he was able to pull up the same radar display Roca had seen.

"No! Wait!" he shouted. "We shouldn't land there!"

Roca was fighting with his stick, wrestling to keep the Accuser's nose up.

"Why not?" he shouted back.

"Because there's nothing there." King shouted. "We'll be stuck. We're better off heading towards the mainland. Get as close as we can and ditch."

Roca grimaced behind his helmet's faceplate. A new, even more urgent alarm began to flash on the panel to his right and he glanced down at it.

"Too late now," he said. "We just lost the other engine. Brace for impact."

CHAPTER 11

Stromer found the others gathered at the rear of the med-block. There was a gap between the block and the north wall of the base, a long passage that was out of sight of most of the rest of the camp. Even though it was early in the day, Sword Base was already unpleasantly warm, and the gap behind the medblock was shaded from the sun's attention too. It was the perfect place to go for soldiers who did not currently have any assigned duty and did not wish to have one given to them.

Without a sergeant or a lieutenant, the unit would not be going out on any more patrols. Until they were reinforced or, more likely, folded into other depleted units, they could look forward to being assigned only the most menial and unpleasant duties to be found on the base.

Not that this was necessarily a problem for Oneyul and Vallow. Both of them wore loose-fitting medical smocks and both were officially confined to the medical quarters until released by a docbot.

They had scrounged up a collapsible metal-framed chair and Oneyul sat in it with one leg stretched out awkwardly in front of her. Wrapped around her thigh was a micro-dermal cast that glowed with a soft red light as it applied sub-microwave stimulation to the damaged tissue beneath. The wound she had taken at Almar Square had turned out to be a compound fracture in her femur, something that had only become apparent when she collapsed with the effort of getting Vallow, her fire-team partner, from the base's landing pad and into the medblock. Even with the cast, the docbot's opinion had been that it might take four days for the bone to fully recover.

For his own part, Vallow had taken a hit to the arm, a Veer-myn energy ray that had torn into his left bicep. While the wound itself was not classified as life-threatening, he had lost a significant amount of blood in the square and he had leaned on Oneyul nearly all the way from the Enforcer's ship to the medics. Now that he knew that she had done this for him, supported him while carrying her own broken leg too, he had been practically unable to stop apologising to her.

A pile of supply crates had been built up against the back of the medblock and Vallow perched on the edge of one of them, facing his partner. His injured arm was cradled in a sling and wrapped in bio-dressings. In his other hand he held a canteen of water.

Beggs sat on a crate above and behind him, smoking one of the awful-smelling and quite definitely contraband cigars he took on every deployment. Both he and Rains were wearing fresh uniforms, though only Rains had bothered to put armour on top of his.

The newest member of the team still stood slightly to one side of the others. He no longer felt like, nor was he being treated like 'the rook'. But the battle at Almar Square had affected him deeply. Of all the survivors of Almar Square, he was possibly the most wounded.

"Thought I'd find you part-timers back here." Stromer said as he approached the group from the barracks-end of the passage. He was smiling as he said it though and he dropped one shoulder, feigning a slam on the much-bigger Vallow as he got close to him. Vallow gripped him around the neck with his right arm, but with the canteen still in hand, and the other limb bound as it was, there was not much else he could do.

Oneyul smiled too as she watched the pair grapple.

"Actually, we were all surprised we didn't find you back here before us. Put him down, Vall, he's liable to break."

Vallow let the struggling Stromer go and he stood up again, giving the bigger marine one last soft punch to his uninjured arm before he nodded a greeting to Beggs and Rains.

"Nah, not me," he said. "Indestructible, me."

He was trying hard to affect a casual and light-hearted air and the others went along with it. But they all knew they were lucky to be alive and that for some of them the danger was not yet over.

Stromer sighed as he took a swig from Vallow's canteen. The sun was nearly directly overhead now, negating, at least for a while, the shade in the passage.

"Hell of a night, last night." he said, handing back the flask. Vallow grunted in agreement but the others stayed silent. Beggs puffed out a smoke ring.

"Hell of a night." Stromer repeated.

"Any word from them?" he said as he handed back the canteen to Vallow. Oneyul shook her head.

"No. I heard their ship take off at first light this morning. Beggs, you hear anything?"

Beggs had his face up to the sun and his eyes closed, like a lizard soaking up heat. The scar around his neck was clearly visible as he puffed out a mouthful of smoke.

"No." he rasped. "I heard from a tech in the bunker they were nearing the Hilton. But that's all."

"I don't like it." Stromer said.

"What?" Oneyul asked. "The Enforcers being here or the fact they took King with them?"

"Both." Stromer replied. "It's a typical Core-job though. They come out here and take whatever they want and the rest of us just have to put up with it. No offense, Rains."

Rains shook his head. "Hardly any taken."

"Well, for what it's worth, I don't think it was quite as one-sided as that." Oneyul said. She was trying to adjust her position in her chair and having some difficulty getting comfortable thanks to the big cast. She waved Vallow off as he moved forward to help her, a concerned look on his face.

"What do you mean?" Stromer asked.

Oneyul gave up struggling with the chair and sat back again, resigned to her own discomfort.

"Well, we saw King in there last night." She flicked her head towards the morgue unit on the end of the medblock. "He came in after he'd dropped off our 'guests' with the commandant. I think he wanted to say goodbye to the sergeant and the others. But he seemed to think it was as much the boss's idea as the Enforcer's."

"Oh, yeah? The commandant put him up to it, did he?" said Stromer. He thought it over for a moment. "So what do you think Patrin's up to? I mean, there has to be an angle in it for him somewhere."

Vallow leaned forward.

"The commandant is an officer. But he isn't stupid. King

134

wouldn't talk about it, but if I had to guess, I'd say he's the commandant's spy. Commandant wants him with them so he knows what they're up to. You know what he's like. Thinks this world is his world. Hell, he thinks this company is his company. He just hates that there might be someone here that knows more about what's happening than he does. This way, he can keep tabs on them."

Stromer was impressed. Vallow had never been the most talkative marine in the unit, but the big man's tactical analysis of the current situation seemed on point.

"That would make sense, I guess." Stromer said. "I mean, if anyone's as sneaky as a Core-worlder it's the commandant. Again, Rains, no offense."

Rains shook it off again but up on his crate, Beggs was grinning.

"Well, damn him all the way to hell," Stromer said. "If anything happens to King, rank be damned, family be damned. He'll answer to me."

"Oh, hell!" Oneyul whispered. "Incoming."

Stromer's eyes flicked up and then followed Oneyul's. He cursed quietly too as he realised they had been discovered. Approaching them from the same end of the passage Stromer had used was the Commandant's Second in Command, Major Corrick.

Corrick was, as ever, dressed in his full battle uniform, but he held a large datapad folded under one arm. He marched briskly towards the group, barely giving them time to scramble to attention. Beggs had somehow managed to make his cigar disappear before sliding to the ground beside Vallow, though the cloud of blue smoke it left behind was somewhat harder to conceal.

If Corrick noticed it though, he did not mention it.

"Falcon squad, good." he said as he reached them. "Just the people I was looking for." said Major Corrick. "Saves me a lot of legwork finding you all gathered here together. At ease, at ease."

He looked over the group, scowling slightly at the sight of the injured Oneyul and Vallow. His face broke into a broad smile when he looked at Stromer, Beggs, and Rains though.

"Good," he said again "Good. I see you are all without an NCO this morning. Just because you find yourself without an NCO this morning, doesn't mean there isn't work for you to be doing."

"Yes, sir." said Stromer. As much as he resented being given any duty, it was hard to dislike Corrick for handing it out. Stromer had served under him for some time and knew the major was a real soldier, despite his officer's rank. But he also knew that if he had only arrived in the passage behind the medblock a few minutes later, he still might have avoided him.

Corrick pulled the datapad out from under his arm and began to pull up the schedule for work that needed to be done around the camp.

Before he could say another word though, a sound like a particularly violent thunderclap ripped through the air above Sword Base.

"What the hell?" exclaimed Stromer. He knew a sonic boom when he heard it and he scanned the skies around them, shielding his eyes with one hand as he did so.

A shout of alarm came from the walkway that ran around the inside of the perimeter wall above them. A pair of patrolling marines were pointing and shouting at something somewhere on the far side of the medblock.

The remaining marines of Falcon and Major Corrick had

to run to the end of the passageway to see what it was. This time Vallow supported Oneyul's hobbling progress.

It was still some way off, but the orange ball of fire racing towards them was unmissable against the pale blue sky.

"What is it?" Rains asked. "A meteor?"

Stromer shook his head.

"No. Too big."

The fireball was growing in size as it got closer to the base and now they could all hear it too. The sound of straining jet engines was unmistakeable.

"It's a ship." said Corrick.

"It can't be." said Rains. "It's too low."

More of the base's personnel had joined them now, spilling out of the maintenance sheds and the second block of barracks at the south-west corner of the base. All of them were craning necks as they watched the approaching mass of flame and metal.

It was on them in seconds and there was a moment of shadowed darkness as the ship passed them, almost directly overhead. Stromer had no idea what its altitude might have been, but it felt as if the giant ship was close enough to touch as it roared past the base. The ground shook beneath their feet and he heard glass breaking somewhere behind him. It was moving so fast, he only caught a fleeting glimpse of its structure – long and thin, with some kind of outer framework attached to it – but he knew what it was.

It was a cargo hauler, one without any cargo attached.

Then it was gone, lost to the sight of all but the sentries high up on the wall as it continued its apparently uncontrolled descent towards the seas on the far side of the base.

The marines within the compound were dazed, shocked both physically and emotionally by what they had just seen.

Rains turned to Corrick.

"Was that the –?" he began. His voice trailed off though, as if by not saying it he could make what they all feared they had just seen somehow not true.

But the major was already walking away, his head down as he marched towards the command bunker, the datapad firmly clenched beneath one arm again. Oneyul and Vallow were limping away too, back towards the medblock entrance. He looked around for Stromer, but the corporal was nowhere to be seen amongst the crowd of onlookers. Rains was alone with his partner.

"Was it?" Rains said. "Was that the Hilton?"

Beggs looked him in the eye.

"That was the Hilton." he whispered. "That's where they took King."

CHAPTER 12

The Accuser had come to rest at the water's edge. Its rear end, including the loading ramp to the passenger bay, was partially submerged beneath the gently lapping waves but flames still burned half-heartedly around the shattered engine housing. Its fuselage and wings were streaked with black soot and pockmarked with scars where it had been struck by loose parts of the Hilton. But it was upright and it was intact.

A hatch on the side of the passenger bay swung open and Forward Observer Roca stepped out and into the sunshine. The ship was canted at a slight angle and he had to jump down from the lip of the hatch, splashing into the knee-high water before striding up onto the beach. He had taken his helmet off, but the filters built into his enhanced eyes shaded them from the glare of the sun as he turned and scanned the sky.

The Hilton was gone though. All that was left to see of her was a dissipating smoke trail that ran towards the distant mainland. Most importantly, the trail passed over it.

"Well done, Sergeant," he said quietly. "Your service is noted. You have done their will."

He heard a noise of movement from within the Accuser. He looked down to see King emerging from the same hatch he had just used, looking shaken but not seriously hurt.

Power within the ship had gone out before they hit the ground and the marine squinted in the sudden sunlight. He stepped down from the hatch and through the water before falling to all-fours when he reached the relative solidity of the pebbly beach. He tugged the chinstrap of his helmet loose and threw it down beside him.

He lay back, feeling the hard stones on his back, the warmth of the rising sun soaking into his tired bones. It felt like he had been on the move for weeks. There were trees beyond the beach and he could hear the song of birds somewhere amongst them. The soft rattle of the stones beneath the Accuser mingled with that of the waves washing around it. He could smell the salt of the sea.

The battering his body had taken during the re-entry and the descent, not mention the sheer terror of it all, had taken a toll. He could imagine lying where he was for a very long time.

He heard Roca then, crunching across the pebbles back to the shell of his ship and, after a few minutes inside, splashing back up onto the beach. King sat up, grimacing at a new pain he had discovered near the base of his spine.

Roca was carrying two small black crates, one in each armoured fist, and he set them both down on the beach. He had been carrying his long rifle slung over one shoulder too and as King watched he pulled out the weapon's power pack and discarded it before sliding in a replacement from a pocket on his belt.

The Enforcer nodded towards the two crates.

"First box is food. Ration packs. They're probably a bit

more bland than the ones you're used to, and higher calorie count, but they're still good. Just don't eat them all in one go. The other is survival gear. There's a shelter, cord, that sort of thing. I've set an emergency beacon off in the ship, but there's no way of knowing how long it might take someone to get to you out here."

King was confused.

"Ok, that all sounds great. But, what the hell are you talking about?"

Roca was testing the sights on his weapon, aiming it towards the distant trees to check its range-finder against his own estimates.

"Survival gear. For you. To survive with."

"Yeah, I get that," King said. "But what about you? I mean, where do you think you're going?"

Roca lowered his weapon. The sun was almost directly behind him and King had to shade his eyes with a hand as the Forward Observer stared down at him.

"The ship's radar picked up some buildings a few clicks inland from here, just before we landed. I'm going to go check them out, see if there's a way off this island. You're going to stay here and wait for a rescue party."

King shook his head and wearily climbed to his feet. He grimaced at the pain in his back.

"No, no, no," he said. He bent over and picked up his helmet. "No way you're leaving me here. Not now. Not like this."

Roca's face was impassive.

"This is not open to debate," he said.

"You're damned right it's not!" King exclaimed. Roca shifted his stance slightly and King held up a placating hand.

"Look," he said. "I get it. You're the Enforcer. You're the 'Will of the Council' and you've got rank and authority and all that crap. You've got your mission and you have to carry it out. I understand that. But look, I've got a mission too. For better or for worse, my orders are to stay with you. You know that. And besides,"

He turned and looked up to the skies, towards Guiders City. The smoke trail from the Hilton was nearly completely gone now, just a few wisps of white on the azure blue.

"I think your mission is becoming mine now too."

Roca slung his rifle and looked towards the treeline above the beach.

"You'll slow me down." he said.

"Well," said King, "Yeah, maybe I will. Or maybe I'll surprise you."

They stood in silence for a moment before Roca started walking, his boots crunching up the stony slope.

"Yes," he said, "Maybe you will."

"So, Roca said, "Any idea what we might find up here?"

They were walking in single file with Roca leading the way through the thin trees and scrub bush that seemed to cover the island. The Enforcer had found some kind of game trail, a thin thread that wound uphill from the beach and into the island's interior.

"Not really," King said. "Shouldn't be anything. There's a few small islands like this out here, but I don't think they're inhabited. Too small to do anything with."

He stooped and pulled up a long strand of pale calico grass and bundled it into his mouth. It was an old bush trick he had learned as a boy – the grass tasted slightly bitter as he chewed it but it got his mouth watering. He had already drained the last of the fluids from the bladder on his back and held little hope they would find a fresh source any time soon.

"I think I remember hearing about some exploratory drilling work out here years ago, but nothing panned out. 'Chert', I think they called it. Too hard to drill through efficiently so they just built mobile rigs or went inland. And Acreon's not exactly a popular tourist destination. Not a lot of pressure to build anything out here."

The Enforcer grunted acknowledgement, but King couldn't tell if he was agreeing with this assessment or not.

"So tell me about yourself." Roca said.

King spat the wad of calico out and started looking for another fresh strand.

"What do you want to know?"

The Enforcer might have shrugged, it was hard to tell with the heavy armour he wore.

"Anything, I suppose."

King smirked at the Enforcer's back.

"Why? I thought you people already knew everything about everyone."

Roca shook his head. "No. Not everything. A lot, but not everything." He half-turned towards King and smiled. "And you're all that's left of my team now so I want to know more."

That surprised King. Until then, the Enforcers had always seemed self-assured to the point of arrogance. Even Mouse.

Roca kept walking but he checked the readout on his wrist unit, confirming their position relative to their destination.

"Your Commandant told me you were born here?" he said.

"Yeah, that's right." King said.

"And you left Acreon to join Drakenhof?"

"No, not at first anyway." King waved off a redfly that was trying to land on his face. "Not by a long way. I did a few other contracts with some smaller outfits first. A few local jobs across Ariadne. Colony work mostly, a couple of small wars. Nothing major."

"But enough to get their attention."

"Yeah," King agreed. As one of the most prestigious security consultancies in the western GCPS, a contract with Drakenhof Marine was not easy to come by. The company liked its recruits to be proven operators before it committed to their further outfitting and training. "Can you believe I signed on with them because I wanted to see more of the galaxy?"

"And they sent you –"

"Right back here," King finished. "Back to this dry rock. And now here I am following you to who knows where because my commandant ordered me too."

Roca laughed then, a low dry chuckle.

"Theirs not to reason why," he said.

"What's that?"

"Theirs not to reason why," Roca repeated. "It's a line from an ancient poem. Dates back to Sol. It goes, 'Theirs not to reason why, theirs but to do and die'. The poem is about some soldiers sent on a dangerous mission not of their choosing."

"Huh," said King as he pulled a fresh piece of calico grass and folded it up. "Sounds about right. Anyway, it was pretty much unavoidable that I'd be a marine."

"Why's that?" Roca asked.

"Family business." King said as he chewed. "My dad was a soldier when I was born. Actually earned his place out here as a reward for his service. For all the good it did him."

"Does he still live here?" Roca asked.

"No," King replied. "He took one job too many. Ended up on the wrong side one day.

"He took a job with a bunch of mercs operating as free-lancers in the Persid sector. There had been trouble brewing out there for a while. Two big corporations throwing their weight around, both of them trying to be the big business out there. Both of them appealing to the Council to recog-nise their rights to a few balls of rock circling a gas giant.

"Well, eventually they did. My dad was on the side they decided had to lose. So they sent in the Enforcers."

They walked on in silence for a while then. The only sounds were the rustling of the wind in the trees above them and the occasional buzz of an insect flying past them.

"Persid is a long way from here." Roca said eventually.

"It sure is." King agreed.

They had turned off the trail that had led them from the beach and now they were descending the other side of the hill. King could see the trees getting thicker ahead of them at the bottom of the slope.

"Tell me about Acreon then." said Roca.

"There's not that much to tell, really." King said. "It's officially a fourth sphere world, but really not much any impressive because of it. Settlers first got here, what, eighty G-standard years back, sponsored by some big Core company."

"Reiker." Roca interrupted.

"Yeah, that's right." King lost his train of thought for a moment as his mind drifted back to the Hilton and some-thing he had seen on the bridge there.

"Anyway, obviously the planet didn't really pan out like

they wanted it to. I mean, it's M-class, but only barely. The settlers settled, but they still might not have made it if it weren't for Briotek."

"Why's that?"

"Well, without their financial support Guiders City would probably have been abandoned a long time ago. They built the farm towers, you know? I think the original plan was for the tech to be deployed to other colonies, I don't know if it ever was though. But having them here, their money, it kept the place going."

"Interesting," said Roca. "I'd never heard of Briotek before I came here."

"Yeah?" said King. "Must be thousands of companies working leases out here. Can't know them all."

Roca nodded. "Yes. Maybe."

They walked a few more paces in silence. The sun was nearly directly overhead now and King could feel sweat running down his back. They were nearly under the cover of the trees he had seen earlier and he hoped the air would be cooler in their shade.

"Ok, I give," he said. "What's up with Briotek owning this place?"

Roca stopped then, standing beneath the thin branches of a very dry-looking tree. He looked around and back up the hill, as if he were taking stock of the terrain.

"Well, it might be nothing. But I think there are some things that just don't add up."

"Like what?" said King.

"Like you." Roca said. "Drakenhof Marine. Your company is one of the best private security enterprises this side of the galaxy. The Drakenhof's don't come cheap and they don't come easy. So, if this planet is what you're saying it is, a barely surviving colony world, supported by technology not being used anywhere else you know of, then why is a corporation I've never heard of paying for you to be here?"

He looked at King then, fixing him with his pale grey eyes. His face was neutral but King could feel the pressure of his gaze, boring into him. King stared back.

"Ours not to reason why," he said. "Mouse even said something like that."

He nodded towards the shaded area between the trees ahead of them and walked past the Enforcer.

"Come on," he said over his shoulder. "Wouldn't want to slow you down."

They pushed through the trees until they found themselves on the edge of a wide clearing. Within it, across a short stretch of dusty ground that was studded with a few low bushes and young trees amid a light covering of grass, King could see a wide, single-storey building. It was unmarked, plain duracrete with no windows and a single entrance with a heavy metal door facing where King and Roca stood.

"Nothing on the island, eh?" said Roca.

King shrugged. "I told you I'd been away."

He was about to step through the treeline and out into the clearing when Roca grabbed him by the wrist and pulled him back and down.

The sights of Roca's rifle whirred quietly as he scanned the building and the vegetation around it.

"There." he said.

King sighted his own rifle where Roca's was aimed and tried to see what the Enforcer had.

He was looking at the bushes to the left of the building, about halfway between their position in the shade of the trees and the building's entrance, but at first he saw nothing out of the ordinary. He recognised a few different species from his childhood; Thornwood, a short Grief's Oak, all plants you could find on the mainland.

Finally, he saw it.

At the base of the Thornwood was a small box. It was well-camouflaged, but its square corners were definitely man-made. It looked barely bigger than a box of ammunition for his old BG-03, and while most of it had been painted to blend in with the trees around it, its top half was a matt black.

"Networked security sensor." Roca said quietly beside him.

"Networked to what though?" King said.

Roca's rifle fired then, the noise startling and harsh in the quiet forest, and something exploded in the branches of the tree above the sensor. Roca tracked right and fired his weapon again, and then once more. Two more security devices King hadn't even seen exploded in their hidden positions in the vegetation to either side of the building.

Roca looked up from his sights, evaluating his work.

"Gun drones." He said. "Set up to kill anything over a certain mass threshold that came within range.

"Good shooting," King said. He meant it. Had he been on his own he knew the drones would have cut him down where he stood and he probably wouldn't even have heard them coming. "Is that all of them?"

The Enforcer looked straight at him. "I can think of one way to find out."

They advanced towards the building with weapons raised, scanning ahead of them and to each side as they moved.

The sun was high overhead, but King could feel a cold tightness in his stomach as he waited for another unseen security device to open fire on them. But nothing happened. No automated sentry system was triggered, no blaring klaxon alerted anyone to their presence.

"Are you sure we should be doing this?"

Beside the door was a combination keypad and biometric scanner. Roca had broken the cover free of its housing as soon as they reached it, jamming a long knife between the two pieces of plastic and wrenching them apart. He had then run several wires from a bypass device he had taken out of a pouch on his armour and plugged them into terminals on the exposed circuitry of the lock. A holographic display was running through numerous security combinations and override routines as it tried to unlock the sealed door. King was watching the process from the other side of the entrance's frame.

"Doing what?" Roca said without looking up from the bypass unit.

"Breaking into a locked building." King said. He flicked his head towards the smoking remains of one of the gun drones Roca had destroyed that lay on the ground a few metres away.

"Particularly one clearly designed to keep people out."

"That's partly why I want to get in." Roca said. "We need a way off this island, which means communications with the mainland. I'm hoping there will be some way of doing that inside this building. But there's also the fact that this building seems designed to keep people, particularly people like me, out."

The bypass device emitted a series of angry beeps and King could see red lights flashing on its display. Roca frowned and gave it a new set of commands, his fingers moving lightly over the device's projected keyboard.

"Did you know there are roughly one thousand standard security encryption protocols currently in use by corporations across the GCPS and deployed to secure its facilities? I have been supplied with the codes to override nearly all of them." He looked down at King. "Perk of the job."

He jabbed at the keyboard again and paused as his new command was executed.

"But, for some reason, this lock does not recognise any of them. And when someone goes to all the trouble of installing gun drones and using security protocols not recognised by a senior representative of the Council of Seven, that tends to make me a little, shall we say, curious."

King looked over at the Enforcer's device.

"But you can't get us in."

Roca's fingers flickered over at the keyboard once more and after a moment the device chirped happily. King stepped back at the sound of heavy motors engaging in the building behind him. The door began to slide open.

"There's nowhere I can't get in." Roca said as he folded the bypass device's wiring away.

CHAPTER 13

The lift doors slid apart with a pneumatic hiss, the light within the car flooding out into the darkened corridor beyond. The descent had only seemed a short one, but Roca and King stepped out into a scene from hell.

The lift opened out at the junction of two long hallways that extended away at right angles into flickering darkness. The lighting built into the ceiling panels was still functional in places but in others it had been cracked or shattered. The only noise they could hear was the occasional shorting of electrical circuits, sparking and fizzing from somewhere ahead of them. Scorch marks peppered the walls and beneath them lay dozens of bodies.

Most of the dead they could see were wearing hazmat suits, but the thick, rubbery white material was ripped and torn and splattered with blood. Some even still wore all-enclosing headgear with wide transparent panels, attached to rebreather units on their waists by thick rubber tubing. But there were also several more bodies dressed in grey combat fatigues under heavy armourweave plates.

Roca knelt down beside the nearest of the uniformed

bodies and reached beneath its shoulder to turn it over. It was a male, human, with several bloody lacerations across his face. A high-powered assault rifle lay on the floor beside and the armour on his chest was cracked where some kind of energy weapon had burned through it. Roca noted the quality of the man's equipment, his dark skin, the lack of facial hair beneath his blood-smeared helmet. He estimated he had probably been around forty G-standard years of age when he died. Certainly no recent recruit. But there was no insignia on the man's uniform and no name badge either.

"One of yours?" he said to King. The marine was looking over his shoulder, his eyes wide, as Roca held the fingers of his left hand to the chestplate of the dead man's armour and made a mental note of the separation between the pen-etrating scorch marks.

"No." King shook his head as he looked along the cor-ridor beside him. "No. Not Drakenhof. I don't think so, anyway. ADP, maybe. I don't know."

"Well, somebody paid them to be here. And something killed them."

"Maybe we should ask him."

King had taken a few steps along one of the two hallways and was looking through the doorway of the first room he had come to. Roca stood and walked over to him.

The room he was standing outside of was some kind of scientific laboratory. Workbenches lined the walls but most of the assorted glassware and machinery on top of them was broken or shattered. Draped over a high stool with metal legs that stood just inside the room was a dead Veer-myn. It still clutched a bulb-ended ray-gun in one clawed fist but the back of its armour bore several penetrating burn marks. Its tail hung down limply, resting in a pool of dark blood that had formed around the legs of the stool.

Roca looked over the bodies laying near him, the corridors stretching away on either side.

"Ok, we split up. Look for survivors. Look for a way to contact the mainland. Looks like we missed whatever happened here, but stay alert. This one could still have friends down here."

Roca moved quietly, his footsteps barely audible above the background hum of the few pieces of machinery he could see that were still working. He had found several more lab-spaces and a few offices on either side of the corridor he had chosen to sweep and although they all seemed well-equipped and maintained, most bore the scars of violence. The glass partitions between several of the rooms had been shattered and more broken glassware lay scattered around damaged electronics and electrical machinery. There were many more bodies too.

He stopped at each one to check for vital signs before moving on. Many wore the same heavy white hazmat suits but more were soldiers, as anonymous as the first. There were several more Veer-myn corpses as well.

He found two more lying dead in the first room along the corridor and several more as he worked his way along it.

They looked much like all the other Veer-myn Roca had seen in his career as an Enforcer. Tufts of dirty brown and grey hair poked out from beneath roughly crafted and poorly painted plate armour. Some wore helmets, others went bare-headed. All wore ragged clothing around their waists and legs and all of them stank. None of them seemed as emaciated as the ones aboard the Hilton had been.

He could feel his conditioning trying to take over at even

the sight of an alien threat but he forced it back down as he analysed what he was seeing. He recorded what he saw on his helmet's camera and as he picked his way through the carnage he made notes of blood trails and where the walls were marked with weapons fire.

Seeing patterns and extrapolating their outcomes was a large part of his training and purpose. In war he had been taught to recognise the ebb and flow of battle, to see how troops were moving and performing, to predict the outcome of each skirmish and engagement and then give orders that would achieve the optimum outcome for friendly forces. But the battle here had already been fought – and lost – and he was trying to piece together how, and why it had started.

Every body and bloodstain was like a piece of a puzzle, but one he had to complete in reverse. He knew what the final picture was, how the story ended. The Veer-myn had killed everyone in the place and lost some of their own along the way. But where had they come from? How had the separate pieces all moved into place? Why had the Veer-myn attacked here?

He was just outside the doorway of another blood-soaked laboratory and about to enter it when the sound of clinking glass came from the end of the corridor to his right. He had slung his rifle but he swung round with his pistol drawn, ready to meet whatever threat presented itself. This time he let his combat-conditioning take over.

He held his position for a moment, tense and ready to fight, but he heard nothing more.

He was standing outside a pair of heavy swing doors and slowly, with his pistol at the ready, he pushed through them and into the darkened room beyond.

***

King had to use the flashlight attached to the barrel of his rifle. Although the power in the subterranean complex was still functional, many of the lights in the rooms on either side of the hallway he was working his way along were damaged or destroyed completely.

A familiar sense of unease, one that had been pleasantly absent during the walk across the island's surface, had returned. He had been tired after they left the Accuser, and by no means relaxed or comfortable, but being outdoors, beneath the trees and the sun had felt familiar and natural. Now though, as he poked his way through laboratories and office spaces filled with the dead, the feeling of being watched was back.

The numerous Veer-myn corpses he had found along the way had not helped.

He had found at least a dozen of them, all ragged and gruesome, but, most importantly, dead. There were more of the grey-uniformed soldiers amongst the bodies as well. He checked them all, not expecting to find name tags but thinking there was a chance he might recognise one of them, maybe an ex-Drakenhof man or someone he had fought with for another company. None of them were, but then he already knew they wouldn't be.

He hated lying to Roca. Deceiving him. But orders were orders. This planet belonged to the Drakenhofs, just like he did. At least for now. And their business was their own. He knew and respected that. It was part of the deal, what he had signed up for when he took the company tattoo.

So why did it feel so wrong?

He was being cautious as he moved along the hall. Even if he didn't know from first-hand experience that there certainly could be monsters lurking in the dark, he had seen enough bad promo-dramas to know that poking around on your own at the scene of an alien attack was a dangerous practise. So, he didn't go all the way into the next room, but held a position at its doorway and carefully scanned it with the beam of his flashlight.

It was a dormitory, a long, low-ceilinged bunk room with beds for at least a dozen. The next room was the same.

"What the hell were you all doing down here?" he asked the empty rooms.

Further down the hallway, on the opposite side, he found another dead lab worker sprawled half in and half out of a laboratory. The lighting was still functional in the lab and he could see a long, heavy-looking table in its centre with chrome edges around its smooth white surface. Work-benches laden with racks of tubes and odd-shaped glassware lined the walls and warm red lights glowed within what looked like a small oven to his right. Three huge specimen jars, sealed at the top with metal rings, lay on the bench opposite. They seemed to glow too, but there was a more sickly, greenish-yellow tint to them that put him in mind of something he once saw happen to an Elastopod in the Thunderball Championships. A black case, made out of some kind of hard plastic lay open on the table and at the far end, hanging from the ceiling, were the shattered remains of some kind of computer monitor. He knew he should walk on by, continue his sweep and then get back to wherever Roca was, see if he had found a way to contact the mainland. But something about the dead woman held him there.

The lab worker or scientist or whatever she had been appeared to have been shot in the back, judging by the burn marks he could see on her suit. He wondered if she had been running away from her attackers or whether they had surprised her as much as they seemed to have surprised the soldiers that had been contracted to protect them. He wondered who she was, where she had come from. Whether anyone would miss her now she was gone.

He decided to pull her all the way out of the lab so he could perhaps try to lay her to rest with something like a little more dignity. He was bending over to do so when he heard something, a soft scraping sound, like someone trying very hard to move without being heard.

He reached behind himself quickly, unslinging his rifle and bringing it up to his shoulder. His breath was catching in his throat and his heart hammering in his chest as he prepared to fight for his life.

But there was nothing there. No Veer-myn leaped out from behind the table or skittered along the darkened corridor to shoot him with their ray guns or stab him with a knife. The lab was still empty, the technician at his feet still dead. But he knew he had heard something.

He took a step inside the lab, his grip on his rifle never loosening as he tried to remember the room-clearance protocols that had been drummed into him on one of his first ever training courses with Drakenhof Marine.

Roca switched the optics on his rifle to infra-red and aimed it into the hole. He had already measured it at nearly three metres across and now he could see the tunnel behind it running down and away from the complex. It was almost perfectly round, though the edge of the hole on his side was slightly ragged where whatever machine the Veer-myn had used to make their assault had broken through.

He was in what he had made out to be the complex's

common or eating area. It was a large space with room for maybe a hundred people to occupy at once, though he doubted it ever did. The wall to his left was almost completely taken up by various vending and rehydration machines, and rows of benches and low tables lay broken and scattered across the pale blue floor behind him. There were numerous bodies too, both human and Veer-myn.

The floor itself was littered with shattered plasteel and duracrete and much of it was cracked and broken. He had recognised the pattern left by the tracks of heavy vehicles at once.

Some of them were still there. Two strange-looking mono-wheels lay on their sides near the hole. He had checked their engine blocks and found them still slightly warm, but he could only guess which of the Veer-myn corpses lying around them had been their drivers.

They weren't what had made the breach though. He had followed the reversed trail of puzzle pieces here and found the tunnel entrance in the canteen. Its interior looked smooth, but when he reached out a hand to touch it his glove's receptors told him there was a slight grain to the stony sides. But he already knew there would be.

The Veer-myn were fond of using tunnelling vehicles, massive motorised contraptions fitted with rotary drilling gear, as both underground transports and ambush vehicles, and they had obviously used one to get here from the mainland. Then they had simply driven it through the wall.

He doubted they could have done so quickly though, particularly if what King had said about the hard rocky foundations of the islands on this part of the planet was correct.

Now that he had all the pieces of the puzzle he could see

how the Veer-myn assault had played out.

The Veer-myn had made their breach and killed everyone they found in the canteen, including the security force. It had been a fierce battle though – the two monowheels had been stopped even though both had heavy weapons built into their sides. Had there been more resistance than the Veer-myn expected, perhaps? But still, the assault force had moved on and into the rest of the complex, destroying everything they found along the way. He couldn't know for sure, but judging by the size of tunnellers he had seen before and the number of dead he had counted, by the time they turned their assault vehicle around and sent it back along the tunnel to the mainland, he guessed most of the Veer-myn assault force must have been killed in the effort.

It was unusual behaviour for the Veer-myn in more than one way.

Background material on alien races was supplied to the Enforcer corps by ETCU, the Exo-Threat Counteraction Unit. ETCU was tasked with studying all alien lifeforms and developing the technology and techniques necessary for the GCPS to overcome them, and Roca had memorised practically all the data they had on Veer-myn.

He knew how they bred, that every nest had a Brood Mother to whom most, if not all the other Veer-myn were genetically related and fanatically loyal. He knew they had a talent for mechanical and biological manipulation and that their populations were larger and more widespread than most people in the GCPS would believe possible. But he also knew they were a secretive race, one that preferred to stay hidden from the societies in whose shadows they lived.

They were elusive and shy, unwilling or unable to enter into normal relations or communicate with other races, including mankind. They hitched rides aboard corporate spacecraft and lived on refuse and cast-off machinery and tech beneath settlements. And, while outright theft by Veer-myn was common, they only rarely stole enough to warrant a colony or ship's crew putting together a party to thin their numbers.

At least that had been the pattern of their existence until recently.

Roca had read the reports from Exham, heard about the takeovers in other systems too, uprisings that had warranted the execution of new Containment Protocols to put them down. It was the difficulty Enforcer groups had found in executing these Protocols, or at least adapting them from their original target, that had drawn him to Acreon in the first place.

The Council was interested in all reports of Veer-myn activity now, how they fought and where and why and, of course, there was a certain prize all Enforcer personnel had been alerted to obtain if at all possible.

The word amongst his fellow Observers was that the Veer-myn were changing, or at least their behaviour was. Something had spooked them and they were coming out of the shadows on dozens of worlds and systems.

Like here.

He looked again at the wrecked vehicles, the dead bodies, the blood trails and discarded weapons.

They had come here for something, something valuable. Something that, even though they had met some fierce resistance, they would not leave without.

They had fought their way past the junction, past the lift shaft, so he knew that whatever they had come for, it was on King's side of the complex.

There was the mystery of the grey-uniformed soldiers too. There were too many of them for a place this size, too many for day to day security work guarding a population of scientists and technicians. The quality of their arms and armour meant they would have been a formidable threat to anyone that attacked them, let alone a Veer-myn raiding force. So who had they been expecting?

He was still mulling over the implications of the things he had found when he heard the sound of laser fire from some distance away in the compound. Then he heard King yelling into his comm-link.

He found him in a lab at the far end of the complex. His rifle lay on the floor beside him and he was on his knees, struggling and trying to pull something big and white out of a large, low cabinet set into the wall on one side of the doorway. There was another corpse laying across the room's threshold and as Roca carefully stepped over it, his pistol drawn, he could see there were several still-smoking scorch marks on the cabinet's metal shell.

"I nearly killed her!" King said. Roca could see now that the marine was trying to carefully lower to the ground the bloodied body of a person he had found hidden in the cabinet.

It was a woman. She wore the same white hazmat suit as the rest of the scientific personnel wore and it too was torn and stained with blood. But she was alive, and she groaned as King helped her sit up, her back to the closed side of the cabinet in which he had found her.

She was young, Roca saw, but tired, and her face was pale and drawn. A dark clot of blood ran from her short black hair onto her right cheek and from the way she held her arms tightly together over her stomach he could tell she was hurt there too.

King kneeled down beside her and pulled open the small med kit he carried in a pouch on his belt.

"I checked out nearly all the rooms along here," King said, pulling open a packet of antibacterial wipes. "There's some dorm-rooms, loads of bunks. Not the greatest accommodation I've ever seen, but you could live with it." He threw away the now-bloodstained square of fabric and pulled a sealed dressing pack from kit. "Then I came in here. I thought I heard something. Then I saw those – those things over there. And when she moved in here, I, well…"

His voice trailed off but Roca read the embarrassment in it anyway. It was clear what had happened. King had come into this room, on edge, expecting trouble. He had seen something that had unnerved him even further. Then, the woman hiding in the cabinet behind him had moved, startling King enough that he nearly shot her. Now he was doing his best to see that she stayed alive.

Roca stepped past the two of them, intent on finding what it was that had first attracted King's attention. He scanned the room, seeing at first only piles of the same kinds of equipment he had seen elsewhere in the complex. He stopped when he saw the large glass sample containers on the far bench.

There were three of them, each one a tall cylinder, with metallic bands at each end holding them tightly sealed. A faint hum told him there were electronic safety measures built into them, the kind that were only used to transport the most dangerous biological materials.

As King tended to the woman, Roca stepped closer to the cylinders, feeling his combat conditioning trying to take over. His subconscious already knew what he was see-ing but he held it back. He needed to be completely sure.

The cylinders were filled with a viscous fluid – air bub-bles were still visible, trapped in the green-tinged material. Within each container were parts of a body.

One held the lower part of a leg, a left one with the foot still attached. The shattered end of a fibula was visible, pok-ing out of bloody flesh. The next one was a forearm, three fingers missing from its hand. The third appeared to be a rib with chunks of raw flesh still attached as if the bone had been torn out if its owner roughly. Each piece was still rec-ognisably human, but they were different too.

Much of the skin on the two limbs appeared to have been flayed or stripped off. What was left of it was covered in large blisters. Some appeared to have popped, leaving cra-ters in the skin, rimmed with hard, bone-like material. They looked like satellite scans of meteor strikes on a moon. The digits were all stretched and misshapen with long, claw-like nails. There were bony protrusions too, sticking out like spurs through the skin of the arm and the leg, and the rib he saw was much wider and thicker than a normal human rib ought to be.

The samples in Markham's lab were all infected with something that had mutated them into sick parodies of humanity.

Roca's lip curled in distaste but there was one final con-firmation to be found of what his conditioning was already telling him was true.

There were labels attached to the top of each cylinder, plastic strips that had been marked with a black pen. He could not see all of them and so slowly, carefully, he reached out and turned the middle container around. It was heavy, and the humming intensified slightly as Roca gripped the top of it, but the fluid inside did not move when he turned it around.

The label read, 'Sample #894, Nexus Psi'.

He put the sample back down and slowly turned back towards King and the woman he had found.

King had finished dressing the survivor's head wound and now he was looking towards her abdomen, as if he was considering whether or not to cut open the hazmat suit and see how bad the rest of her wounds were.

There was a large black case on the table. Next to it was a data tablet. Roca picked it up and keyed it on. A security screen appeared on the device's display, demanding a password that he didn't have. There was a symbol at the top of the screen though, one that seemed familiar. Roca let his enhanced memory do the work as he tried to place it. It was a face, a woman's, but in the place of hair she had what looked like a nest of writhing snakes. It was a stylised depiction of something from a very ancient story he had read once. Then it came to him.

"A gorgon." he said, looking up.

King's patient's eyes were still closed, but was that a small flicker of recognition he detected, a minor twitch of her facial muscles when he said the name?

King made a decision and reached over to his med kit for the small field scissors it contained.

"Ok, then, Miss whoever-you-are," he said to his patient. "Sorry for, well, nearly killing you just now. But we're here to help you and everything's going to be alright."

Suddenly, before he could pick up the scissors, the woman's eyes flashed open and her hand shot out and grabbed his wrist. King yelped in pain and surprise. He tried to pull his hand back, but her grip was surprisingly strong. She looked him between the eyes.

"My name is Doctor Everret Markham," she said. "And you're wrong. It's not going to be alright at all. We're all already dead."

CHAPTER 14

"We had been having trouble with some of the electrics all day. A few blown lights, one of the secondary labs lost power in the morning, some flickering circuits here and there. Then the air-con went just after lunchtime.

"We didn't think too much of it. It was unusual, but not that unusual."

Markham paused from her account of the events that had led her to take shelter in her laboratory to take a drink of water from the glass beaker King was offering. He had filled it from a sealed plastic jar he had found marked with the label 'Distilled H2O', miraculously unshattered amidst the carnage of the rest of the lab. Markham was still where he had put her after she had been removed her from her hiding place in the cabinet, legs stretched out in front of her. King kneeled beside her.

Roca had seemed to ignore the doctor ever since he had entered the room. He had taken a look at the gory specimens King had noticed when he first investigated the lab and since then seemed utterly engrossed in trying to break the security on a data tablet he had found on the table.

King could not tell if the Enforcer was even listening as Markham told her story.

"Stuff breaking down?" King said.

Markham nodded and took another sip from the beaker before continuing.

"Yes, things would break down every now and then. A lot of money was spent building this place, but not enough was budgeted for its ongoing maintenance.

"So, I sent one of my junior technicians up into the vent system to fix it. Parnassa, his name was. A good worker. I think he came from Psalmus, or somewhere else in the Core. He never came back from the vents though. I suppose he was the first one they…"

Her eyes flicked upwards and King followed her gaze. He could see the air vent built into the ceiling of the laboratory.

"Well, I suppose they probably killed Parnassa first if he found them up there somewhere." Markham continued. "But the rest of them came just after we had finished work for the day. I think most of us were in the canteen when they broke in.

"The first we knew anything was happening was when the clock fell off the wall. There was a terrific rumbling noise, it got louder and louder, and then, suddenly – suddenly they were in."

"They were horrifying. I never knew they could be so big. Or so vicious." Markham said. She spoke emphatically, like a scientist reporting an interesting observation, but her face was pale and King could tell she did not have long to tell what was left of her tale.

"They must have killed a dozen of the others in the first moments of the attack. The security detail, the men they sent to guard us here, they tried to, they tried to –"

"Fight back?"

She smiled wanly at King.

"To survive. I ran."

Markham sighed as she remembered her panicked flight along the corridor back to her lab, the screams of the people behind her and the ones who had rushed towards the canteen to see what the noise was all about.

"I ran and I hid."

King shook his head. He had seen enough Veer-myn to know that unless you were trained to fight them, running was probably the best option.

He looked down towards the doctor's abdomen. With one hand she held the beaker he had given her, but she kept the other one protectively over her stomach. Dark blood was seeping out between her fingers and pooling in her lap.

"But one of them tagged you." he said.

Markham glanced down, but then she shook her head.

"Actually no. No, it was one of the security detail that did this."

She moved her hand away from her stomach a fraction, revealing the torn flesh beneath it. She groaned with pain and King winced at the sight.

"Your security did this?" he said. Markham nodded.

"One of the guards, yes. When it became clear they couldn't... contain the situation. He killed her too." Markham nodded her head towards the body still laying across the threshold of the room. "Their orders were probably to kill us all if they had to. It was chaos in here though, Veer-myn everywhere, so as you can see he didn't do a very good job. He probably would've finished me off though if it hadn't been for the Veer-myn that killed him first."

"But why?" King said.

"Because they didn't want her to tell anyone what had been going on down here." said Roca without looking up from the datapad.

Markham nodded. "Just another safeguard.'

"But that's crazy!" said King. "They build this place, put you down here, and then kill you when someone breaks in and –"

"Steals what you've been working on." Roca finished. "That's it, isn't it? They came here to steal what you had made."

Markham shook her head, but weakly. "No. It can't be. They cannot be that – that smart."

Roca put the datapad down and walked around the table towards Markham. He knelt down opposite King, the servos in his armour whirring softly as he drew near to her.

King felt a sudden sense of unease then, as if the temperature in the room had quickly dropped a couple of degrees. He could feel violence in the air, the same way he had felt the storm approaching back in Guiders. It was then he realised Roca was still holding his pistol. It hung by his side, muzzle pointing at the ground, but the Enforcer apparently had no intention of holstering it.

He had the same look on his face King remembered seeing when the Forward Observer had asked him about Drakenhof's presence on Acreon.

"The Veer-myn trade on the notion that they are a backwards and primitive race." Roca said quietly. "The fact we know so little about them reinforces that idea. But make no mistake, the Veer-myn are as complex and sophisticated a threat to the GCPS as any other alien race in the galaxy.

"Now, tell us, Doctor Markham, what exactly did they take?"

King could feel the threat implicit in how Roca talked, how he held himself. The Enforcer's armoured form seemed to fill the room, taking up all the space between himself and the doctor as he stared into her eyes. Even then, despite Roca's imposing presence, for a moment King thought Markham might refuse to answer his question. A flicker of defiance flashed across her face but Roca did not back down or move away from her. If anything he seemed to grow bigger as he knelt by the wounded doctor.

Finally, Markham looked away from Roca, though whether through shame or fear King could not tell. When she opened her mouth to speak her voice was barely more than a whisper.

"You know what they took."

Roca scowled at Markham.

"How much?" he growled.

Markham looked at King, taking care not to meet Roca's gaze as she turned her head.

"Corporal, I wonder if you would tell me how many of the six vials of material I placed in my case on that table are still there, please?"

King stood and looked. Inside the black case was a foam layer with six cut-outs, each one of them about as long as his index finger and twice as wide.

"You mean this empty case right here?" King said, lifting it up for Markham to see. The doctor nodded.

King felt the tension ramp up again and for just a second he had the distinct impression Roca was considering killing Markham on the spot. It was hard to tell from where he was standing, but he thought he saw the Enforcer's weapon twitch – just a little. Roca didn't fire, but he didn't holster the weapon either – as if Roca had needed to fight an instinctive reaction.

"Wait, wait, wait!" King said, holding his hands up. "Now does anyone want to tell me what we're talking about here? Can we all just take a breath and talk this out, please?"

He looked at them each in turn, silently pleading for some reason, a pause in whatever it was that was going on between the two. Roca looked up at him as if he was noticing King for the first time.

Roca stood up then and took a final look at Markham. Then he walked back round to the far side of the table and set his weapon down upon it. He picked up the tablet that he had been working on before interrogating the doctor. King took a deep breath.

He looked down at the doctor. She looked more tired than ever now and the pool of blood in her lap had grown larger. There was still some strength in her though and she looked up at him with kind eyes.

"Corporal, I wonder if you would refill this for me?"

She held up the beaker she had now emptied of fluid and King nodded agreement. He took it from her and walked back around the table to where he had left the water jar. It was on the table near Roca.

King poured the doctor's drink and then glanced back towards Markham. She had closed her eyes again. The only sound in the room was that of Roca's fingertips tapping across the datapad screen. King spoke in a low voice as he began to pour another draft of water into the beaker.

"So do you want to tell me what's really going on here, Lieutenant?"

Roca's eyes lifted from the pad.

"You're asking me?" he said.

"Yes." said King. "I am. You know what they were doing down here, don't you?"

Roca set the pad down and stood up straight. King was reminded instantly how much bigger than him the armoured Enforcer was. He carefully screwed the lid back onto the water jar.

"Come on, Roca," he said. "I saw your face when she started talking about this. When you saw what's in those things." He glanced at the specimen jars and his nose wrinkled in disgust. "You know what it is. So how about you share what you know? It's like I said back on the beach – we're in this together now, whether we like it or not."

Roca considered the marine's words and for a moment King thought he might have pushed the Enforcer too hard. But then he spoke.

"Very well," Roca said. "I do not 'know' any more about this place or its purpose than you do now. But yes, I have an idea what it is they were working on. What it is the Veer-myn took. And I hope with all my heart that I am wrong."

He picked up the datapad again and flicked through the pages he had been able to access.

"If this weapon the Veer-myn have taken is what I think it is, then the doctor here may very well be right. We may be dead already. I have seen – something like this on other worlds. It is very deadly and if it is released it will result in the death of every living thing on this planet."

"Is it an Enforcer thing? Some kind of bioweapon you had made?" King said. Roca looked a little offended.

"No. Not at all. Quite the opposite. It is something the Council has briefed every Enforcer to destroy at all costs and without hesitation. That is all I can tell you and you should believe me when I say it is all you need to know. At least for now."

King started to object but Roca silenced him with a raised hand.

He looked the marine directly in the eye and his face became stern.

"On this you will have to trust me. I cannot and will not tell you any more. This is for your own protection."

King looked away in frustration.

"I understand your anger," Roca said. "That may be hard for you to believe, but it is true. The secrets I keep, I do so for a reason and it honestly is for the good of the GCPS – for all of us.

"But if we're both being honest here," Roca continued, "I think it is probably time you tell me what it is that *you* know about this place."

King looked back sharply at Roca. He was alarmed to find the Enforcer had his hand on his pistol once more.

CHAPTER 15

King looked up at Roca, still struggling to process what he had been told and trying very hard not to give the Enforcer any excuse to use his weapon.

"What do you mean?" he said. "About this place?"

"Yes," Roca said quietly. "When we first came in here. The soldiers we found. Those grey uniforms. You recognised them. I saw it. And back on the Accuser, after we broke free from the Hilton. You were very keen for us not to land here, despite the fact that as a native of this world you must know the waters between here and the mainland are very, very dangerous. So, again, if we are being honest, what do you know about this place?"

King was caught and he knew it but he was faced with an impossible choice.

On one hand was his past and his duty. On the other, the present awful reality.

He had hated the Enforcers for a long time, hated the Council even, ever since his father had not come back from doing his job. His father had died simply because *they* had decided that was the way it had to be. So, when Drakenhof had ordered him to keep the Enforcers away from their business he had gone along with it because of that hatred. It should have been easy – being sent off-world should have kept them all out of harm's way. Yet he and Roca had still ended up here.

He had felt used before, he still did. But he also knew he was only alive because of the Enforcers' willingness to sacrifice themselves too, a sacrifice that meant Guiders City was still standing and what was left of the planet's population was still alive. Now he was faced with a new threat that could kill them all anyway. Unless he helped another Enforcer fight it.

'We're not the bad guys.' That was what Mouse had said. Looking at Markham, the bodies piled up outside her lab and the pieces of monstrosities contained within it, he was starting to think that might be true.

"Alright," King said. He couldn't look Roca in the eye, but he knew it was time to tell the truth.

"Yes, you're right. The grey uniforms. I've seen them before. I've seen them passing through Sword a few times. They come in and out on unmarked shuttles and they never stay long. I figured they were transiting in from an orbiting ship and then heading to some inland operation or something. But now I guess we know where they were actually going."

Roca nodded.

"But to do that, to use your camp, that would mean someone there knows about this place. Someone high up in the chain of command too." he said.

Yeah, I guess so." King said.

And this island?" Roca said.

King frowned.

"No. I didn't know this place was here. I never actually

lied to you. But yeah, there were a few places I was ordered to keep you and your team away from and this island was one of them. But I swear they never told me why."

He looked up, looked around himself at the ruined lab, the rooms beside it.

"I had no idea this place was here, what they were doing. I just thought – well, I don't know what I thought really."

He looked away from Roca then, at the floor, at the broken glass under his feet. A mixture of shame and embarrassment flushed his face. But when he looked back up he was defiant.

"I know what you did, you know."

Roca looked puzzled.

"What *I* did?"

"Yeah," said King. "Back in Guiders. I know you used us. As bait for that thing. The Progenitor. When they told me to keep you reined in, I guess I was mad enough to agree to anything."

Roca said nothing, confirmed nothing. But he did put the weapon back on the table. Then he picked up the datapad again and stared at if for a few seconds. Then he looked back up at King.

"This makes sense now." he said.

King stifled a laugh.

"Oh, really?" he said. "How does any of this madness make sense to you?"

"This." Roca said calmly. "This is what you're here for. This is the answer to the question, why Drakenhof?" Roca gestured towards the lab, the neighbouring rooms.

"What do you mean?"

"This place is what you're guarding." Roca said. "Not Guiders City, but this. This is why your company was contracted and so quickly. I wouldn't be surprised to find there's been a retainer in effect for a long time, actually. It could be your company was always on hold to come here or wherever something like this happened."

King felt a surge of unease rising from his stomach but Roca was not finished.

"Your company came to fight the Veer-myn. But what would happen if there were a Veer-myn invasion that were not dealt with swiftly? Who would be called in to deal with it?"

"You would." King said. "The Enforcers."

"Yes, we would. And we would shut this planet down tight. Nothing would be allowed in and nothing would get out until we were satisfied it was completely purged. We would leave no stone unturned. And that would very definitely not be good for whoever set this place up."

King was beginning to understand exactly how much he had been used. How much of the suffering he and his unit had gone through had been simply so someone else could use Acreon, his home, as their own personal black site.

"You think Drakenhof is part of this. Part of 'Gorgon'?" he said.

"Maybe not all of them." Roca said. "The mission here is genuine enough. But the answer to the question of why a high-price mercenary outfit would send several hundred and women to protect a fringe investment nobody seems to want to claim ownership of is a simple one – so nobody else would."

King's head dropped. The enormity of what he had learned, of what Roca was saying, seemed beyond belief. He knew he had to focus, to keep his mind on the here and now.

"Ok," he said. "This is big. Horribly big. And I wish you luck trying to figure it all out. But right now, the biggest question I have is this: what the hell are the Veer-myn going to do with whatever it is they took from her?"

He pointed towards the doctor.

She was still where they had left her, sitting with her back to the cabinet, and her eyes remained closed. But something had changed. One of her hands rested in her bloody lap but the other hung loosely by her side. Next to her open hand lay a small micro-injector, the same design the docbots at Sword Base used to administer antibiotic solutions and painkillers.

"What in the Core?"

King rushed around one side of the table towards the doctor while Roca went the other way. In his haste to reach her, King nearly tripped over the body of the dead worker that had first drawn him into Markham's lab.

"What is this?" he shouted, picking up the injector. He turned it over, looking for a label, some clue as to what it had contained but it was blank.

Roca gently cupped Markham's face in one giant hand, lifting it up. Her eyes opened slowly, wearily, as if she was having trouble focusing on the Enforcer's face.

"What did you do?" Roca said.

"What I had to." Markham whispered back. "I'm not a monster. I don't want this thing released on this world. I know how terrible that would be. But I won't risk being here, still alive if it is."

Her eyes focused on Roca. "And I won't be dragged back to the Core by you either."

King threw the injector away in disgust. Roca watched it fall but he held onto the doctor.

"Opiates?" he said.

Markham closed her eyes again, as if she were drifting off to sleep.

"Correct," she said. "I should have died with the others when the Veer-myn attacked. But I've corrected that mistake. The opiates I just injected myself with will stop my heart. Very soon. And when I die, so will you. This whole place has a safeguard for that. None of us are getting off this planet but at least we won't become one of them."

"One of who?" said King.

"Very well." Roca said, ignoring him. "Perhaps you're right. But know this: I will report what I have seen here, what this place is and what you have done here to the Council. I will find out exactly what Project Gorgon is and the people responsible will be punished. You have my word on this."

Markham opened her eyes for the last time and she smiled sadly as she looked at Roca's earnest face.

"My poor deluded Enforcer," she whispered. "Do you really believe some of them don't already know?"

King was sure he could hear the cleaner device warming up in the ceilings above him as they ran. Every rattle, every sound of sparking circuitry, he was certain meant fiery annihilation was about to be released onto him and Roca.

"Are we sure about this?" he shouted. Roca was ahead of him, leading them back along the hallway towards the lift shaft. They were nearly there now but Roca was showing no sign of slowing.

"Oh yes." he shouted over his shoulder. "Honestly, I'd be surprised if there wasn't something pretty horrible up there getting ready to wipe this place out. Keep moving."

King jogged to a halt.

"But the lift is this way –" he said, pointing to the open door.

Roca kept running. "We're not taking it." he shouted. The Enforcer turned a corner and King ran after him, taking care to avoid the bodies that lay across his path.

"Then where are we going?" he shouted at Roca's back.

"Back to the mainland," Roca called, "Back to your camp."

King caught up with him in the canteen. He looked around in shocked amazement, taking in for the first time the bloodshed and destruction.

"Ok, so what are we doing in here?" said King, trying to catch his breath again.

"You asked before what the Veer-myn would do with the bioweapon they took from this place. I think the answer lies in their nature." Roca said as he walked towards the hole in the far wall. "They're not completely animal, but they are still largely ruled by their instincts and this makes them highly territorial, especially when provoked."

King snorted at that.

"Provoked? They attacked us! They invaded Acreon."

Roca raised an eyebrow. "Maybe, maybe not. But if they went to all the trouble of stealing whatever they were working on here, I think it only makes sense that they would have a plan to use it against their biggest threat. Their biggest enemy."

King sighed.

"Ok, let's say you're right. Obviously we have to do something about it. But what? How the hell are we going to get back to the mainland in time to stop it? Why are we still down here when we're both sure this place is getting ready to kill us as soon as that crazy doc back there dies?"

"Well, I have an idea. But you're probably not going to like it."

King followed the Enforcer's gaze but it took him a moment to realise what he was seeing. Then he looked at Roca as if the Enforcer had gone mad.

"You have got to be kidding me." he said.

The pneumatic whirr of the bolt-fastener filled the Brood Mother's inner chamber. There were dozens of bolts studding her battle armour and each one had to be affixed individually. Three junior Maligni attended her, joining the heavy plates across her stomach and back, over her head and around her thick thighs and arms. Slowly and methodically they were sealing her within its carapace. Next they would need to bolt on the massive power-plant, the device that would make her a truly deadly titan of war. It was a long and time-consuming process, but the Mother did not mind. The voice had told her the end was near and she wanted to be ready for it when it came.

A chorus of hisses and screeches came from the far end of the chamber, echoing from the roughly-carved stone walls. She looked towards the entrance, her keen eyes seeing easily through the gloom. It was the raiding party, or at least what was left of it.

She howled with displeasure as she watched them approach, loud enough to make her attendants pause in their task lest she lash out at them in her anger. She counted less than half the number of her children she had sent on the mission to the human's secret weapons factory. A handful when she had sent a small army.

But their leader still lived. The Malignus with the stubby ear and the mechanical eye. He approached her throne, his tail held low, his head slightly inclined to show her his throat, his respect. His armour was scorched and burned, but he still lived.

She beckoned him forward and he came. He was carrying something and he held it out before himself. She leaned forward to see it.

Six glass vials, each one filled with a thick, almost clear liquid lay in his palms. She sniffed at them, suspiciously. She could smell humans, the faint odour of their world, but no danger.

She looked behind her at her litter where it lay on her bed, wrapped securely in warm blankets, and called to it softly.

After a moment it answered her in the voice only she could hear. Yes, it said, this is the weapon we sought.

She turned back and cooed softly at the one-eyed Malignus. He was more clever than she had suspected, certainly moreso than the humans could have.

His network of spies had led him to their workshop buried under the island a long time ago and he had patiently watched them there ever since. He had recognised some of the symbols the humans used to mark their equipment, particularly the signs that meant 'danger', painted on glass jars in heavy stasis boxes, delivered to them from another world. Even if he had not, he understood the meaning of the elaborate precautions the humans in the white suits took whenever they handled them.

He had his own laboratory in the nest and he knew a thing or two about contagious diseases.

He had understood the general principles of what the humans were doing, even if he did not know the specifics or the provenance of whatever disease they were trying to reverse-engineer and refine. They were, to his Veer-myn eyes, very clearly making a biological weapon, one that they feared greatly. It stood to reason that this was something that could be turned against the human soldiers in their own high-walled nest. The Tangle had seen it in his mind and it had agreed with him.

The Malignus grinned at the Mother's display of affection.

Most of the nest, all her children that had survived the war, first with the interlopers, then with the humans, had assembled in the chamber now and the air was filled with the sound of their anxious hisses and squeals. They sensed the time was coming for the final battle.

She looked at them, their eyes meeting hers, and she told them they were right.

When the others had come, the strange Veer-myn without a nest and without a Mother of their own, they had started a conflict the Brood Mother had not wanted and would never have sought. They had been forced to destroy the invaders, fighting them above and below the surface to protect their territory, the colony the Mother had worked for so long to establish, and they had won that battle. But the damage had been done - they had attracted the attention of the humans and started an even more dangerous war.

Now they had a means to end it. The vials the Malignus had captured would enable them to kill all the human soldiers and make it so they would never come back. The nest had not started the war, but they would most certainly finish it.

There was but one more battle to be fought.

As her children screeched their approval and squealed their willingness to do anything for the Mother, her attendants resumed fastening her into her armour and lifted the power-plant into its place on her back. Then she sent them out. She dispatched all her remaining children to their vehicles, the last tunnellers the nest had left, and she ordered the Maligni to bring out their most deadly weapons. Nothing would be held back for this final confrontation.

As her army streamed out of her chamber and she prepared to join them, it called to her.

She went to it, her footsteps accompanied by the soft pneumatic hisses of her powered armour. She nuzzled the bundle of rags that held her litter, letting it smell her and know she was there. But of course it already knew.

She asked it if it would be enough. Her army was still strong, but she had lost so many children fighting the invaders and then the humans. What if they were too few?

The bundle quivered as if the thing within it were cold, though she knew that could not be the case. Her chamber was always the warmest place in the nest.

Finally it answered her.

Yes, its tiny voice said. There were enough of her children remaining to end the war. Because really, all that was needed was one.

CHAPTER 16

"Damn Corrick. And damn Stromer too." Rains said. The winds were whipping up and over the perimeter wall and he wiped sandy grit from the corner of his mouth. "I'd pay my entire bonus to see either of them up here right now."

Corrick had found the two of them again in the mess hall shortly after lunch. He had refused to answer any questions, other than to confirm what they already knew – that the ship they had all seen streaking overhead that morning was indeed the Hilton – and this time he had wasted no time in setting them both to sentry duty. Of Corporal Stromer there had been no sign in the mess though, and neither Beggs nor Rains had been able to tell the major where their teammate was.

So, it was only the two of them that Corrick had sent up onto the perimeter wall that evening. It was dark now and desert-cold and Rains and Beggs were high up, patrolling the walkway around its inner edge. To Rains, it felt like they had been on duty for months now. The glowing timepiece on his wrist told him they were barely halfway through their four-hour shift though.

Beggs said nothing. He knew both men, Stromer and the major, were both only acting according to their nature. Corrick was a soldier. A professional. Not a particularly bad one either. But he understood the importance of discipline in a military force and, as much as he hated being up on the wall with Rains, Beggs could appreciate that. He had been many things before joining Drakenhof Marine and lived a life without discipline and it had nearly ended him. But joining the company had changed him. Made him a soldier too.

But Stromer... The man was good in a fight, but Beggs doubted he was really made for life in a private military. He might change – anyone could, he thought to himself as he looked at Rains walking beside him. But he had a fairly good idea where the corporal was this evening and, if he was right, it was probably the best place for him for the time being.

They were walking along the northern wall and nearing the guardhouse in the tower at the north-west corner of the compound when Beggs stopped and cocked his head to one side.

Rains stood next to him and he raised the scope of his rifle to his eye. He turned slowly, scanning across the sandy ground outside the camp's walls, past the guard tower and towards the few distant lights of Guiders City to the west.

"What's up?" Rains whispered. "I can't see anything. You hear something?"

Beggs didn't say anything at first. Then, after a moment, he shook his head. "No." he said. "Just the wind."

The younger marine lowered his rifle.

"Come on." said Beggs. "Only another couple of hours to go."

***

188

Oneyul was in the infirmary where she was supposed to be. Officially she was resting, but she was bored almost out of her mind.

She lay on her back half in and half out of her cot, the leg with the cast on laid out flat. The other leg was bounced agitatedly up and down on the corner of the cot's springy foam mattress. A video unit hung from the ceiling on a flexible armature at the end of the bed and she was watching a rerun of a classic 'Ball game.

Still, boredom crept around inside her. Her leg itched under the glowing cast as it applied stimulation to her bone, forcing it to rapidly knit and heal. The boredom was like that, only its itch was in her head.

Vallow was asleep in his own cot on the far side of the 'bay, his arm still wrapped in dressings, snoring quietly. She listened to him snore for a few moments. Then she looked over at the wheeled unit next to her bed, sizing up the contents of the tray an orderly 'bot had placed there before retiring to its charging station for the night. There was a metal bedpan there. It looked heavy but she thought she could probably still hit Vallow with it if she tried.

She hated being stuck in the infirmary. She wanted to be somewhere there was some action.

Stromer picked up his glass and considered the dark brown liquid within it. Japeth, the unofficial manager and chief distiller, had told him the liquor was made using an old Grogan technique. It had a hazy, misty quality to it, like it was constantly shifting from a liquid to vapour and back again, as if it was uncertain which state it ought to stay in. It shifted in his vision as he watched it. But then again, he was so drunk, almost everything in the small but perfectly illegal bar in the Number 3 maintenance shed was a little bit blurry.

He knocked back the liquor in one gulp, relishing the feel of it burning all the way down his throat.

"To Lieutenant Ammit!" he shouted as he raised the empty glass into the smoky air of the bar. A chorus of voices echoed the toast. The place was busy tonight, with at least a dozen other late-night drinkers scattered at tables around it. Most of them hadn't known Ammit, but they understood the sentiment.

Stromer slammed the glass back down onto the rough wooden bar and gestured to the corporal manning the other side.

"One more." he said.

The technicians had built the little drinking den Stromer had camped out in for most of the day almost as soon as they had set up the rest of the base. First they had walled off about a hundred square metres of private space at the back of the shed most distant from the command bunker. Then they had built the bar and installed a few tables and seating, all made with parts commandeered from vehicle spares and building materials. A few hanging strings of LED lights had been the finishing touch. But before all that, they had set up the still and it had been producing good liquor ever since. Those boys were prepared, Stromer thought as his glass was recharged. They knew how to run a war.

Drinking on deployment was officially forbidden and the bar was the camp's worst kept secret – sometimes the noise coming out of the place was so loud you'd have to be stone deaf not to know what was going on in there. But the brass never touched it. And Stromer knew why.

On any long contract there would be days when the

grind of military life would start to wear even the best soldiers down. There would be days too when good marines would be lost. There had to be somewhere for those they left behind to go and remember them. Somewhere they could go to knock back a few homebrews or a measure or two of whatever illicit alcohol they had managed to smuggle into the theatre. A place where they could raise a glass to the honoured dead and tell stories about them and the things they had done, or were going to do. A place to get ready to go out and do it again the next day, knowing that tomorrow night they might be the ones being toasted.

Stromer picked up his refilled glass and raised it up above his head.

"To King." he said.

Beggs was about to open the guard room door when he stopped and turned suddenly. He turned and looked out across the desert towards Guiders City again. Rains halted beside him and the two stood in silence as the cold desert winds swirled around them.

"Beggs, man, what now?" said an impatient Rains. He could feel his toes starting to go slightly numb in his light and uninsulated boots.

Beggs raised a hand and cocked his head to one side.

"This again?" said Rains.

But Beggs didn't move.

"You hear that?" he whispered, his voice barely audible.

"Hear what?" Rains said. All he could hear was the wind, the faint hiss of sand blowing in against the walls and roofs of the camp, and, from somewhere, the sound of other, luckier marines, drinking and toasting.

But then he did hear it. Or rather felt it, even with his

half-numbed feet. A faint rumbling, like heavy machinery operating in a distant room.

The two men looked at each other and unslung their rifles. Rains was about to switch on his night optics again when he felt the walkway shift slightly beneath his feet. He reached out to grab Beggs's elbow to steady himself but both men stumbled as the walkway suddenly rocked sharply underneath them, threatening to throw them to the ground nearly four metres below.

"Into the guard tower!" Beggs shouted hoarsely.

"What the hell?" Rains shouted. He felt a wave of heat as something exploded loudly on the far side of the western wall. With a shriek of tearing metal, the compound perimeter started to collapse.

Vallow sat bolt upright in his bed, his eyes wide in the darkened room. The only light came from the bio-monitor panels above each of the eight beds in the medbay and he struggled to adjust to the gloom for a moment. The lights cast faint shadows across the bay, over its floor.

His heart jumped as he realised there was something on that floor. It was an indistinct shape, roughly man-sized, but wrapped in some kind of rags. Instinctively, he reached for a weapon with his uninjured arm, searching for something, anything to defend himself with. His hand found a metal bowl by the side of his bed and he raised it, ready to strike whatever horror was crawling across the floor towards him. Then the dark shape shifted and seemed to roll in place before letting out an awful but quite recognisable noise.

"You wanna get your worthless arse out of that bed and help me up, you damned malingerer?" Oneyul hissed.

Vallow gulped and replaced the metal bedpan before

he hastily threw off his blankets, the movement awkward using only one hand. He slid out of his bed and stepped over to help Oneyul untangle herself from her own bedding, a sheet and a thick blanket she had somehow become wrapped up in.

"What happened to you?" Vallow said. He was still feeling groggy from the pain meds the docbot had given him and was confused as to what exactly had woken him up.

"Didn't you hear it?" said Oneyul as she pulled herself upright, using the edge of her bed for support on one side and Vallow's uninjured arm on the other. "Massive bang, the whole room shook! Sounded like it came from the west wall."

Vallow shook his head as Oneyul shook off the arm he had used to help her up. The end of the room nearest the doors that led out of it was taken up with storage lockers for the personal effects and uniforms of its patients and Oneyul hobbled towards it as fast as the cast on her leg would allow her to.

"A bang?" said a still confused Vallow. "Like what?"

Oneyul had her locker open now and was pulling her fatigue jacket on. She gave her uniform trousers a suspicious look, like a student evaluating a particularly difficult engineering problem. Then she pulled her combat knife from its holster on her webbing that hung from a hook in the locker and began to slit the left leg of the trousers from hem to knee.

The unmistakeable sound of an explosion came from somewhere in the distance outside the medblock and the lights in the wall panels dimmed even more before they heard a mechanical grunt from beneath their feet as an auxiliary generator kicked in. The lights stayed on but now they could hear marines shouting outside the medblock. Then they heard energy weapons firing – lots of them.

"Like that." Oneyul said. "Now stop standing there gawping and help me get these blasted trousers on."

Stromer staggered out into the night air, his uniform as much a dishevelled mess as his head was. He knew he had drunk too much, more than he really should have. That was nearly always true. But the burst of adrenaline that blasted through him as he left the maintenance shed bar was turning out to be a pretty powerful counter to the effects of all the alcohol he had consumed.

The interior of Sword was normally lit twenty-six hours a day. The massive solid fuel generator installed near the base of the ATC tower ran constantly and supplied power to most of the base's support systems, including the lights built into the perimeter wall and hanging from fittings on the exterior walls of each of the main buildings within the camp. But none of those lights were lit now and most of the camp lay in darkness.

He could smell burning though and the orange glow coming from the far side of the tower told him what at least one of the loud noises he had heard from his stool in the bar had been.

The main generator had exploded.

But it was not the only thing that had gone wrong in Sword. He could see more flames ahead of him, from the direction of the perimeter wall, but any thoughts of some kind of mechanical failure evaporated in the night air when he heard the sound of energy weapons firing too.

Men and women were running past him, most of them uniformed marines, some of them armed, others not. He

grabbed hold of one of them, a young soldier in full combat armour who seemed to be heading towards the flames
at the northern edge of the camp.

"Hey, wait, what the hell's going on?" Stromer asked as
the marine spun around.

His face was pale in the moonlight and he seemed barely
less confused than Stromer was.

"We're under attack!" he shouted. "They're coming in
through the walls! Thousands of them!"

Then he was gone, leaving Stromer trying to figure out
who 'they' were and, more importantly, where he had left
his weapon.

The first marines to reach the breach were the patrol units
that had been walking the perimeter wall on either side and
they were greeted with a scene of utter destruction. A gap
nearly ten metres wide had appeared in the western wall –
two whole sections of Shensig tiles were simply gone and
what was left of the walkway hung limply down, twisted
and deformed.

At the base of the breach was a deep pit, partially filled
with a tangled mess of shattered durasteel and plastics and
the guards approached it at speed, using the thin beams of
the flashlights attached to their weapons to search it for survivors. A marine officer, the senior man on watch duty that
night, began barking orders to the soldiers as they arrived,
but his words were cut short as a flurry of yellow energy
rays burst through the breach.

Other, heavier guns added the weight of their fire to
the volleys too, and the marines were blasted apart. More
chunks of durasteel fell from the perforated wall as the gap
was widened even further.

With a harsh shriek of primal challenge, scores of pale bodies clad in rusted metal armour rushed into the breach, skittering rapidly across the broken ground, pausing only to fire a shot or two at the stunned marines within.

The battle of Sword Base had begun.

CHAPTER 17

Oneyul had taken a knee, bracing her rifle across it as she lined up her shots. She fired slowly, taking her time, making as sure as she could of getting a kill, or at least a hit, each time. This kind of fighting suited her.

She and Vallow had somehow, between them, managed to dress and arm themselves – her hobbling around on one leg, he using only one arm. The docbot had automatically activated at the sound of their movements and had frantically tried to stop them, warning them that it was against protocols for patients to discharge themselves in the middle of the night. It held a nominal rank of captain, despite being a bot, and it had even threatened them with disciplinary action if they did not both immediately return to their cots. So Oneyul had threatened it with a single shot to its artificial brainpan and the docbot had been forced to concur with her assessment of the situation.

Now they were crouched outside the medblock entrance, facing the massive hole that had appeared in the compound's western wall and Oneyul was finally enjoying herself. While Vallow watched her back, she was killing Veer-myn.

She squeezed off a shot, watching the beam fly away into the night through her high-power scope until it neatly decapitated a Nightcrawler that had been about to shoot another marine at almost point-blank range.

The ground between the medblock and the broken outer wall was a frantic melee of marines and Veer-myn. Somehow, despite the lights, the cameras, and the soldiers patrolling the wall, the Drakenhof troops had been caught unawares. They were well-trained though and dozens of marines had responded to the sound of fighting at the perimeter. But with numbers and surprise on their side, Oneyul could tell stopping the Veer-myn at the breach would be a hard fight.

She fired twice and two more Nightcrawlers died squealing. The shots were becoming more difficult as the battlefield became more crowded with marines.

She tried to target a particularly vicious-looking Veer-myn, a brute of a thing with a savage jaw that hung open beneath black animal eyes. It was larger than a 'crawler and instead of attacking with clawed hands it bore two massive wedge-shaped weapons, one slung under each huge fist. In the monochrome view of her sight, Oneyul was sure she could see the things rotating, like massive screw-heads. They were shredders – mining equipment adapted and repurposed into savage tearing close-combat weapons.

Oneyul's shot was obscured momentarily as a grenade round, launched from somewhere to her rear, exploded in her scope's field of view and she eased up on her weapon's trigger. She stayed fixed on the point she had last seen the beast, but when the smoke cleared she winced as she saw it lunging forwards to impale a marine with both fists, disembowelling its victim in a spray of viscera.

It dropped the dead marine then, shaking the corpse from

the shredders, its tongue lolling from its open mouth and a kind of dead curiosity in its eyes. Oneyul took her shot, breathing out and squeezing her trigger, but she cursed as the beam ricocheted off the massive creature's armoured shoulder. The shot seemed to shock the shredder-thing back into action. It leaped backwards and then it was gone, lost in the crowd as dozens more Veer-myn surged forwards through the wall.

Suddenly she heard shouting from up on the wall to her right. The voice was familiar and she looked up from her weapon to see Beggs and Rains on the walkway. Beggs was kneeling, shooting down into the Veer-myn at the wall but Rains was standing. He was pointing down and past Oneyul, past the medblock and towards the open ground between it and the vehicle pool.

She turned around, just in time to see the ground buckle and shake before erupting upwards.

With a roar of engines suddenly unburdened by the ground it had dug through, a massive vehicle burst up from the crater. It was a squat cylinder with caterpillar tracks running along its underside and three whirring drill bits mounted on its front. It reared up as it cleared the hole, its nose pointing towards the sky like a breaching whale, before gravity reclaimed it and it crashed back down to the ground, sending a cloud of dirt and dust up into the air.

Its tracks were still spinning and it rolled forwards, the huge treads screeching and rattling until it came to a halt. Two more of the tunnelling vehicles came after it, each one belching thick fumes from the exhausts built into their hulls and shaking the ground as they shuddered to a stop.

Then they opened up. The drill bits on each vehicle's front swung apart and from between them streamed dozens of

Stalkers, Veer-myn like those the unit had faced in Almar Square.

Some began to move towards the medblock but others fanned out into the camp, disappearing from sight in order to ambush the marines rushing to defend the wall.

The camp had been breached twice now and Oneyul knew its defenders were well and truly on the back foot. She checked her rifle's ammo gauge – it was nearly half-way depleted.

"Vallow," she called. "Aren't you getting tired of being out-manoeuvred by Veer-myn?"

A salvo of screaming rockets suddenly streaked across the battlefield from Oneyul's left and into the Veer-myn trying to run through the breach in the compound wall. Dozens were blown over by the detonations and for a moment the Veer-myn assault was blunted, robbed of its momentum as the raiders already in the compound dived for cover, and those still outside the base held back. The marines closest to them took the opportunity to withdraw too, most of them running back towards the medblock where they could regroup and properly defend themselves. For just a moment, Oneyul began to think they just might carry the fight.

But then she saw the big beast again. It barked and snapped at the more timid Veer-myn around it, even striking some of them where they lay huddled amidst the ruins of the wall. Its methods were different to those Oneyul had seen her own officers use, but the effect was the same – the Nightcrawlers started moving forwards and into Sword Base once more.

She took a deep breath as she aimed her rifle at the monster with the drilling fists, trying to ignore the noisy rush of battle all around her. Calmly, carefully she squeezed the trigger. This was what she was trained to do and she did it very well.

Stromer was beginning to regret ever taking the Drakenhof tattoo. He had almost reached the end of the chain-link fencing that marked the side of the vehicle pool and beside it several heavy-weapons teams had set themselves up, using piled sandbags to form small redoubts. Behind them they had mounted three 'Screamer' MML-09 missile launchers and were sending a wave of missiles towards the breach in the wall. The missiles had lived up to their name, screaming as they flew through the air before exploding in showers of hot shrapnel and forcing the Veer-myn down.

But the invaders had their own heavy weapons too.

Through the gap in the wall, lit like a nightmare by the strobing energy beams and explosive detonations of fire coming from the medblock to Stromer's right, came two large vehicles. Each of them had the familiar makeshift appearance of Veer-myn technology, with huge bulbous wheels that had clearly been pilfered from a corporate mining outpost somewhere out in the desert and thick armour plates that bore more than a passing resemblance to those Stromer had seen bolted on to the side of marine Mule trucks.

The weapons on the back of each vehicle were all Veer-myn though.

One looked like an enlarged version of the ray-guns the Nightcrawlers carried, with a focusing chamber near the end of its barrel and two bulbous metal ammunition reserves above its power plant. The other looked even more outlandish with a wide funnel-shaped barrel with multiple perforations. Instead of power packs, the second weapon had two massive steel chemical tanks attached to its base and Stromer's blood ran cold as he realised what kind of horror the Veer-myn were bringing to bear.

Bright streams of white and blue laser energy were flashing all around the two weapon platforms but the armour built into their sides seemed to easily shrug off every shot that struck them. Stromer stumbled towards the marines manning the Screamers. The crews were hastily reloading their weapons, and Stromer nearly landed flat on his face beside them as he tripped over the discarded lid of an ammo crate hidden in the darkness at his feet.

One of the spotters looked around the weapon he had been reloading as Stromer hauled himself back to his feet, wiping dust and sand from his face as he did.

"What the hell?" he shouted and Stromer suddenly found himself facing down the barrel of the marine's pistol.

"Put that away, Breen," Stromer said, "You might get someone hurt."

A puzzled look passed over the marine's face and was quickly replaced by one of recognition.

"Stromer? Is that you? What're you doing here? Shouldn't you be propping up a bar somewhere?" he said reholstering the weapon.

"Tell me about it." Stromer grunted. "Look out!"

Behind Breen the two Veer-myn weapons platforms had cleared the breach and were now fully inside the compound.

The marines dug in around and on top of the medblock over to Stromer's right seemed to be the centre of the base's efforts to resist their invaders and he could see the flash from their weapons as they poured all the fire they could into the Veer-myn. But they couldn't stop them all and now the second heavy weapon with its chemical payload had reached firing range.

From where he kneeled, Stromer could heard its firing mechanisms engage. There was a harsh whine of pressure building up, and then the machine fired. From its perforated barrel a spray of bright yellow liquid hissed and fizzed as it arced through the air towards the medblock. Then there were only screams as it struck home. Stromer couldn't see the weapon's impact, but he could hear screaming as men and women, his fellow marines, began to die on the far side of the block.

Then it was his turn to dive for cover. The platform carrying the heavy ray-gun had rotated to face the Screamers and there was an ominous hum that grew louder and deeper as its capacitor drew power from its batteries. The hum reached a screaming crescendo as the weapon finally released a series of massive blasts of energy towards them. The machine shuddered as it spat them out in a staccato rhythm.

The marines manning the Screamers were bolting for cover but they could not outrun the Veer-myn rays. The heavy beams blasted into the marine weapons, slagging two instantly and blowing apart the low piles of sandbags the marines manning them had built. The fleeing crews were hit too, thrown wildly apart by the force of the weapon. Stromer hit the deck and he tasted dirt in his mouth as the screaming wounded fell all around him.

Something heavy and angular hit him on the back and he let out a muffled curse, breathing in more sand and dust as he did so. The Veer-myn weapon had stopped firing though, and he cautiously lifted his head off the ground to see what had struck him. A metre away from him, still strapped into his helmet, lay Breen's head.

"Screw this," Stromer said to himself as he rose to his

knees and looked for a way out. "Screw this all the way back to the Core."

Oneyul swore under her breath as the Veer-myn weapon finished its sweeping movement. It was crew-served and she could see several 'crawlers running around its base and over its upper surface. They were clearly having some trouble making the complex weapon fire again, but she knew it was only a matter of time before it unleashed another devastating blast.

She and Vallow had only just escaped being directly in the path of its first shot, having decided that crouching outside the medblock doors was not the best place to be in the face of a rushing horde of angry Veer-myn. Vallow and another marine, a private from another rifle section, had barged a large waste bin over to the side of the block. Together, the three of them had clambered onto it and from there to the top of the building.

There was a low railing running around the edge of the roof and Oneyul had sat behind it on top of an ammo drum her newest companion had brought to the fight. Her injured leg was stretched out awkwardly to one side of her while her weapon rested atop the rail.

More marines had joined the fight too, officers giving orders and shouting curses. Then the Veer-myn spraygun had opened fire and the shouts had turned to screams.

The noises the dying made were awful, but the stench, a mix of hot acid and burning flesh, had been worse.

The heavy ray-gun had silenced the Screamers over by the vehicle pool too and now it was rotating its barrel back around towards the medblock.

Oneyul checked her rifle's ammo gauge again. It was

nearly out but there were still dozens of Veer-myn forcing their way through the breach in the wall.

"Marines! Get some rounds on that thing now! Fire!"

Oneyul looked up from her scope. The order had come from somewhere on the ground to her right.

"Is that Corrick?" she called to Vallow.

But before her partner could answer, they both heard the percussive 'pop, pop, pop' of grenade launchers being fired. They were firing from the passage Falcon team had used that morning when they were avoiding Corrick himself. A few seconds later came answering explosions as the rounds impacted in the swirling mass of Veer-myn at the breach. A dozen 'crawlers were hit, left bleeding from the holes blasted through their armour. But they weren't Corrick's real target and one of the grenades, a single lucky shot, landed square in-between the chemical tanks atop the spraygun's wheeled platform.

It exploded with a massive metallic bang and the Veer-myn that had been trying to make the weapon ready to fire again were thrown into the air around it. The content of the tanks geysered up before falling back down and covering the nearest Veer-myn in thick acid goo.

Now it was the Veer-myn's turn to screech and howl in pain. The flesh of the Nightcrawlers and Maligni that had been operating the machine melted and ran like over-heated plastic. They dropped to the ground, squealing in agony and clawing at the burning liquid.

A cheer went up from the marines around the medblock, but the heavy ray-gun was still operational and now it was ready to fire.

The pulsing of its power plant built up and it spat out a volley of rays at the medblock. Some of its shots missed, going high or flying wide and clear. But more hit the block square on, blasting chunks from its walls and atomising the marines taking cover beside it. The building shook with the impact but it stayed standing.

Another ray struck the railing along the roof to Oneyul's left, instantly killing three marines using it as a firing position and sending her and Vallow diving for cover. Oneyul cursed again as pain shot through her still broken leg.

They were alive but now they were pinned down. Marines were dying all around them and Oneyul could see no way out. Vallow had pushed himself back up and was about to lift his partner up to her seat when they heard the Veer-myn weapon cycling up once more.

"It's going to fire again!" Vallow froze, apparently unable to decide whether to keep going or throw the two of them back down into cover.

Oneyul glanced up, lifting herself on one arm so she could see the Veer-myn weapon. Its rhythmic pulsing built and grew. But then she heard another, far more welcome sound.

A volley of rockets screamed across the ground from her left, striking against the side of the Veer-myn weapon's wheeled platform, bursting apart in showers of sparks and shrapnel. One of the machine's wheels flew off, crushing a Nightcrawler crouching nearby, but the gun's capacitors were still building up charge.

Something else burst open on the side of the platform, a power relay perhaps, Oneyul didn't know. The damage the rockets had done was enough to make it explode in a bright shower of yellow sparks and then the machine canted over to one side. Its barrel was thrown upwards, elevated above the medblock it had been targeting. The gun's operator was nearly flung clear but he held on to the controls mounted at the weapon's rear. It was his last mistake.

The smoothly building tone of the weapon's capacitors suddenly changed pitch, rapidly rising to an ear-splitting screech. With a flare of blinding white they detonated, sending machine parts and Veer-myn bodies flying outwards.

The explosion was huge and Oneyul shielded her eyes with one hand as the marines all around her began to cheer. The explosion had halted the advance and there were no more Veer-myn trying to get through the breach.

"Who the hell is that?" said Vallow. He was kneeling beside her, aiming his rifle off towards the maintenance sheds and Oneyul stretched out to retrieve her own weapon.

She propped herself up on her elbows and looked through her Accutek scope.

A single marine knelt in the lea of the shed. His uniform was dishevelled and torn and under one arm he held what looked to Oneyul very much like the body of a Screamer missile launcher. He had it on its side, propped up across a makeshift firing platform that seemed to have been made from an overturned bar stool. The missile launcher's barrels were smoking and the marine was grinning as he looked at what he had done.

"That," Oneyul said, "is our very good friend Corporal Stromer."

CHAPTER 18

Within his command bunker, Commandant Patrin was wrestling to stay in control of the situation. He wore his battle uniform, complete with the Drakenhof crest emblazoned across his chestplate. His pistol, a gift from the clan patriarch himself, was strapped to his right thigh and his helmet was clipped onto his belt above it. It felt odd being fully dressed for battle and he hoped it was an unnecessary precaution. But there were appearances to be considered.

He stood before the line of screens that ran around the walls of his command centre, watching the feeds from the few cameras still in operation around the base. Most of them were down and their screens were filled with static. The belief was that the Veer-myn had somehow cut the hard-lines that led into the command bunker, but the wireless connections seemed to be suffering from the same interference that had dogged communications with patrols in the city. The few screens that were still operational were relaying scenes of chaos.

Somehow the assaulting force had managed to evade the electronic security devices guarding the ground around the camp. Veer-myn saboteurs, 'Creepers', were known to be skilled at interfering with corporate equipment and it was likely they had played a part in it. They had cut the controls to the Equalizer cannons too. Then they had destroyed almost twenty-five metres of reinforced wall.

A large number of invaders had been contained at the initial breach, but reports of the arrival of more of them through some kind of underground transport had the potential to sway the battle back in their favour. Above his map table a three-dimensional holographic representation of the camp hovered in the air. Reported positions of Drakenhof troops were marked in green, but an increasing number of red units were appearing throughout the base.

Veer-myn were everywhere, it seemed.

There had been reports of Stalkers trying to break into the ATC and all three of the base's Hornets had been found to be unoperational. The south barracks were reported to be repelling assault parties and there were casualties at both generator stations. Only the armoury and the command bunker itself seemed to have escaped direct attack so far.

Still, Commandant Patrin knew the day was not yet lost. Tactical analysis was one of his greatest strengths – he graduated near the top of his class in both Battle Planning and Joint Military Logistics. His troops had been rocked by the aliens' initial assault, it was true. But he could see several clusters of marines had then rallied quickly and were trying to regain the initiative.

Staff officers were working the consoles around the room, dealing with the garbled and sometimes contradictory reports coming in from the marines fighting outside, and trying to relay orders back. He quickly dispatched one of them to order three rifle units of marines that had mustered at their barracks to reinforce the troops holding the med-block and another to draw flamethrowers from the armoury. Once they had repelled the assault force they would need to burn out any Veer-myn lurking in the tunnels they had dug under the camp.

As the messengers left the room, another junior officer marched towards him and snapped to attention. Patrin returned her salute.

"Yes, Jay?" he said.

"Sir, we've just made contact with the captain of the Genoa." Jay said.

Patrin turned away from his map table and searched the monitors for one that would show him traffic through the space above the planet.

"Oh? They're back already?" he said.

"Yes, sir." said Jay, "They're asking if we need assistance. I, er, I think they're offering to help us evacuate, sir."

Patrin frowned and looked back at his map. The units he had just issued orders were already moving in response. There was no reason to expect them not to carry out their orders and hold the base.

"No." he said. "No. Not yet. Please thank the Genoa for her offer and ask them to stay on station though."

Jay saluted again before marching back to her station. Patrin returned to his map.

"Holy karma," Oneyul breathed. "What in all the spheres is that?"

Nearly three full units of marines had gathered on the roof of the medblock now, carrying an assortment of weapons, and more were gathered on the ground beneath them. Rains and Beggs had joined them too, leaving their exposed position on the wall and seeking instead safety in numbers.

They had held the medblock, defended the breach against waves of Veer-myn invaders. They had even cut down the Stalkers that had tried to assault the block from their tunnellers. But something new was coming now, a monstrosity that made those first waves seem like mere probes.

It was out past the wall, too far for her to make a reliable shot, and approaching from the direction of Guiders City. It was big, much bigger than the numerous Nightcrawlers and Stalkers that walked alongside it. Its rotund form was almost entirely encased in heavy metal armour that had been painted a dull red like old blood. Power relays glowed around its joints and dozens of long curved blades extended out from its collar like a gorget of thorns. More blades decorated the head of the long staff it carried, crackling and fizzing with static discharge. Sometimes it used the thing like a kind of walking stick to support its obvious weight, other times as a goad, swinging it and striking some of the slower Nightcrawlers around it, urging them on towards the marines' base.

Its face was largely hidden beneath a heavy half-helmet that covered the top of its head, but through her Accutek scope Oneyul could see red eyes gleaming with fury.

There was something else behind it, but Oneyul could not get a clear view. It seemed to be a platform of some kind, but not on wheels. This one seemed to be floating on an anti-grav field and was either being towed or pushed by a small gang of Maligni that hurried around it, obscuring Oneyul's sight.

"That is one big mother." breathed Beggs beside her. He had pulled out a monocular and was scanning the oncoming horde too.

"You got that right." said Vallow.

It was not the only monster coming either. Oneyul counted several giant creatures that resembled the Veer-myn but lurched forward on all-fours with it too.

Their musculature and gait was even more bestial than the Nightcrawlers'. Crouched down, each one was still the height of a man and just as wide. It was as if they had grown out of control, their bones become unnaturally long. Their broad shoulders were thick with muscle beneath armour plates and cloth wraps, and long claws extended from each fingertip and toe. Their oversized heads snapped and snarled as they came towards the camp, and long ropes of drool dripped from their savage canine teeth.

They wore armour similar to the Mother's with powered harnesses feeding the weapons that had been attached to their backs. Two carried heavy guns while the others supported arrays of long, sickle-like blades with edges that gleamed in the light of the moon.

Each beast pulled at the end of a long chain leash, barely restrained by the Nightcrawler handlers being dragged behind them.

Oneyul cursed under her breath. The beasts were creatures known as 'Night Terrors' – Veer-myn that had been mutated by their Maligni until they became rampaging monsters. Behind her she could hear other murmurs of discontent. The first waves of attackers had simply softened the marines up, it seemed. This was the Veer-myn's final attack and she was not the only one wondering whether it could be stopped.

"So what do we do?" asked Rains.

"I say we get out of here." said another marine. Oneyul turned and looked him over. She wasn't sure, but he looked like one of the men from Sable, one of those lucky enough to make it to Acreon in the first deployment. His nose was slightly twisted as if it had been broken once and not properly re-set. Oneyul was fairly sure she remembered Broken-Nose telling more than one tall story about how many 'crawlers he had personally killed in those first few days of operations.

"So when they're thick on the ground out there you're the big hunter, but now they're where we live you want to bug out?" she said.

Broken-Nose looked at her reproachfully and even took a step in her direction. He stopped when Vallow rose up beside her though. Oneyul could feel a headache coming on, a mix of dehydration and stress, she figured. If the other marines on the rooftop were feeling as bad as she was, she realised, it was no wonder tensions were high.

"Hey!" Broken-Nose said. "That's not how it is! Come on, look at those things!" He pointed over Oneyul's shoulder. The first of the new wave of Veer-myn was almost on the wall now. "We ain't getting paid enough to deal with that! We need to get out of here!"

He was scared, Oneyul realised, and fear could be highly contagious. Most of the marines on the rooftop were privates and Oneyul wished she had an officer with them, someone to take charge and galvanise them. Someone like King.

"No. We don't. This is where we make our stand."

The voice was familiar but Oneyul had to swivel round on her ammo-drum seat to be sure.

Pulling himself up and over the railing at the south side of the roof was Stromer.

He was barely in uniform – just combat trousers and an unbuttoned jacket – and was covered in a mix of dirt and blood. In one hand he held a short-barrelled laser pistol, in the other a long knife. As Oneyul looked closer she realised the knife was not company-issue. In fact it looked more like a Veer-myn weapon.

Vallow stepped forward and helped the corporal over the railing. Stromer thanked him and then looked around at the assembled marines.

"Look, I know you're all tired, you're all hurt. But where are you going to go? These things are everywhere. Our backs are against the wall here. And I for one am tired of being out-thought and out-fought by these alien bastards.

"We came here for a reason, for a contract." He looked directly at Broken-Nose. "And this is exactly what we're getting paid for. We're professionals and it's time to start acting like it."

"Alright, alright." said Broken-Nose. "So what's your plan then?"

Stromer paused, and Oneyul could tell he was uncomfortable having so many eyes on him, looking for leadership. He didn't shrink back though. He tucked the pistol into the belt of his combat trousers and picked up a rifle, dropped by someone earlier in the battle.

"Put it this way;" he said as he checked the charge left in the weapon, "if we stay here, we die, if we run, we die. And I don't like either of those choices. So I say we do something different. I say we take it to them and kick them out of our base, and off our world! This planet is a pile of dirt at the back-end of space. But it's our pile of dirt and I'm not willing to let some alien rat-monster take it! Now who's with me?"

Oneyul smiled. Something had changed in Stromer and she liked it. He smelled like he had crawled out of a still but at least he was finally acting like an officer. He seemed to have convinced Broken-Nose too, or at least pulled him back from the edge of panic.

Oneyul's head was really starting to hurt now. As the marines began to form into combat teams, she rubbed her temples, wondering if she could send someone down into the block beneath them for some painkillers.

"Alright!" Stromer shouted. "Those who can walk, run, and fight – let's go. The rest of you – cover us from here."

The combat units began to climb down from the med-block roof and Oneyul watched them heading out towards the breach. More marines joined them, coming from the maintenance sheds. She tried to take a quick headcount but the pain in her head was becoming really bad now. It felt as if there was something blowing up in her brain, a building pressure like the kind she sometimes felt when taking off or landing in a Hornet.

She squinted down into the sights of her rifle. She could see Stromer at the breach now. He was turning, shouting something.

She flicked her sights up, towards the massive red creature at the back of the approaching gangs of Nightcrawlers. She could get a better view of it now, possibly even a kill-shot if she was lucky. And if that damned painful buzzing in her head would go away.

The thing that had been behind the Mother was in view now too and she moved her sights over to it, curious to see what else the Veer-myn had brought to the fight.

She regretted it immediately. For the second time that night she tried to make sense of what she was seeing. But then *it* saw her and she screamed as pain washed over her from inside her own mind.

***

"Alright, people, get ready for them." shouted Stromer. They were nearly at the breach now and he half-turned as the ragged collection of troops he had found at the medblock jogged along behind him. "Keep your weapons primed, keep your control. There's a lot of them out there, but that just means there's more of them to kill!"

Some of the marines that had gone with him cheered at that. Stromer turned back and checked his own rifle, a weapon he had found abandoned on the rooftop, was ready to fire. It was, but he still had no real idea what he was doing.

It had all seemed so clear a few moments ago.

Firing the Screamer had just seemed to make sense. It was lying there and it was loaded and he had been so stunned by the impacts of seeing Breen and his men dying in front of him, not to mention the impact of Breen's severed head, he hadn't even thought of the consequences of firing the thing. He had just picked it up, made a mount for it from an overturned piece of furniture that had somehow gotten out of the drinking hole, and pulled the trigger. He had done it as much out of rage as any purposeful or soldierly intention. Actually destroying the Veer-myn gun had been as much as a surprise to him as it had probably been to its crew.

Getting to the medblock had been the logical choice after that. He knew at least some of his friends were there and besides, where better to be when hordes of alien vermin were trying to shoot and stab you than in the building with all the medical supplies? So he had started running, intending to save his skin. But he had still been forced to fight for his life when he ran straight into a skittering Stalker coming the other way.

It had put up a good fight, once the shock of how they had come literally face to face wore off. Stromer was fairly sure that when the last of the alcohol wore off he would be feeling the soreness in his ribs and the scratches on his shoulders. But if that was the worst of his injuries, he knew he would have gotten off lightly. Besides, on top of that, there was really no guarantee he would even outlive the effects of Japeth's Grogan whiskey anyway.

He had already lost several friends on this job and he knew he might still lose others. But he wouldn't let that happen without taking as many of the Veer-myn with him as he could.

That conviction had, somehow, resulted in him leading the charge towards the breach in the camp wall and the Veer-myn assembled on the other side of it.

He could see them there now, dozens of 'crawlers and Stalkers with their tails held high as they prepared to strike.

Stromer slowed as he realised something was wrong. Why hadn't they already attacked? In the time he and his troops had taken to reach the wall he was sure the Veer-myn could have swarmed across it. But they hadn't. They were stand-ing still, almost in a line with their big ugly Mother at the centre, at almost exactly the limit of weapon's range.

Memory and a deep sense of foreboding made him stop. He raised his weapon, using its scope to check out the enemy line. There were 'crawlers and Stalkers and the big beasts he had heard some of the marines call 'Terrors'. And there, beside the Mother, was something else too. Some-thing on a wide floating platform beside her.

At first he took it to be a bundle of rags, almost like an unmade bed and for a moment he wondered if that was what it was. A kind of throne perhaps for the Mother to recline on while her children fought. But it seemed too small and she was clearly dressed to fight.

Then something moved amidst the piled rags on the platform and Stromer saw, to his horror, several small heads appear, shaking themselves free of their coverings and sniffing at the air. There were four of them and they waved to and fro as if searching for something. Then they stopped moving.

Stromer felt a pain behind his eyes, a pain that grew and grew until he was blinking away tears. Then it changed. There was still pain but he also felt a kind of frantic buzzing moving around inside his head as if a thousand flies had all hatched from their eggs inside his skull at once and were now struggling to get free.

He shook his head, swatted at it, trying to jog them loose, but it was no good. The buzzing only increased and the pain grew in intensity too, beyond what he could bear, and he sank down to his knees.

He cried out in frustration, unable to force himself back up or to raise his weapon. Sweat ran down his forehead and dripped from his nose as he tried to fight whatever it was that was happening to him. His legs wouldn't respond but he could look around and he saw he wasn't the only one affected. Most of the other marines were down on at least one knee too. Beggs was crawling towards him while Rains stood with both hands on his knees, being sick between them. Stromer wondered if they were hearing the same thing he was or whether they were all experiencing their own private, individual torments.

The big marine Stromer had seen on the rooftop, the one that had been arguing with Oneyul when he arrived, was still standing and for a moment Stromer thought he might have escaped the effects of whatever it was the Veer-myn had hit them all with. On the way over from the medblock, he had introduced himself as Rames, had even apologised for his attitude. But though he was upright, Rames was shaking and sweating, and Stromer could see blood running from his broken nose.

Stromer tried to call out as Rames slowly turned his weapon around and placed its barrel under his chin. But no words would come. Rames pulled the trigger, instantly vaporising most of his head. What was left of him dropped down stone dead.

Stromer forced himself to look forwards again, feeling as if every capillary in his head was about to explode. He could barely see, barely think. But he knew he wanted to stop the Veer-myn now more than ever.

But the Veer-myn line was moving forwards.

CHAPTER 19

Oneyul tried to shake her head but all she could manage was to blink a few times. She was disoriented and stars were flashing before her eyes. She could barely see through her own tears.

When the pain hit her she had thought she was going to die there and then. It was a pain unlike anything she had felt before – a pain that didn't have any physical cause but seemed to come from every part of her body at once all the same. It was still there, throbbing behind her eyeballs, but it had lessened slightly from its initial blackout-intensity. She felt something wet running beneath her nose.

It was the thing, the Veer-myn thing that had no eyes. She had glimpsed its tiny mess of bodies, just long enough to register the black sockets in its four heads, and then *it had seen her*. And, somehow, it had attacked her.

Vallow was lying on the roof beside her, passed out or dead, she couldn't tell. His hand was still clutching the rifle he had been using. Her own weapon lay next to him where she had dropped it and she guessed the ten or so other walking wounded behind her were similarly incapacitated.

She could see the breach though, through the haze in her head, and what she saw filled her with more horror.

Barely half the marines that had followed Stromer were fighting. Of the rest, most were either down on one knee or lying flat out like Vallow.

Whatever the Veer-myn had done to her, it was doing to them too.

It was not affecting the other Veer-myn though. Their line was steadily advancing towards the base, their ray-guns firing into the paralysed marines. She saw them dying and she knew those still fighting would be soon overwhelmed.

The situation was hopeless and the buzzing in her head was getting louder again.

Only she realised it was not just inside her head.

Eventually her pain-fogged mind realised it was an engine she was hearing, a low, throaty growl coming from the tunnel entrance the Veer-myn machines had made in the ground to her left.

Slowly, gritting her teeth with the effort the movement required, she turned her head. Her heart sank at the thought of more reinforcements being brought through the tunnels.

She finished the movement, sweat breaking out on her forehead, just in time to see another machine burst from the subterranean entrance. It was not another tunneller though, and it did not stop at the medblock.

Instead it turned towards the breach and, as it headed away from Oneyul, her heart rose again.

Stromer was trapped in a waking nightmare. He could not move – his body was frozen and people were dying all around him.

The Veer-myn were moving across the sandy ground that

lay between the base and the city and were close enough now that he could see their dark eyes flashing beneath their crude armour. He could smell their stench, hear the sizzle of the air as the fired their ray-guns at him and his marines. The enemy were utterly inhuman, wild savages that only paused from their advance to occasionally bark and chirp at each other in their strange alien language.

They had already killed some of those soldiers that had come with him. It was only the inaccuracy of the Veer-myn's weapons and the resistance of the few marines unaffected by whatever it was that had paralysed Stromer that had stopped the engagement becoming a slaughter already. But brave as the marines were, they were outnumbered and, now, massively out-gunned. It was only a matter of time until they were overwhelmed.

But they were not the only thing he could hear.

Something big, something mechanical, was coming from behind him, from inside the base. He could hear the harsh note of an engine that had either been very badly tuned or was straining through the wrong gear. There was a heavy rattling noise too, like he had once heard a Forge Fathers' tracked tank make, but lighter.

A cold sweat broke out all over him – the Veer-myn had outflanked them, he thought, sent more troops in through the tunnels. He wanted desperately to turn, to raise his weapon and fire it, to do anything. But it felt like something was inside his head, blocking his mind somehow as he frantically tried to will his limbs into action.

Then the vehicle raced past him.

It was a single huge armoured track with its motor and two passengers riding inside it. Two ray-guns were mounted either side of the riders' seats and thick green exhaust fumes trailed behind it. It was clearly a Veer-myn-made vehicle, but its driver completely ignored the marines.

Instead, the studs on its track-segments dug up great divots of earth as the machine moved past the wall and towards the approaching Nightcrawlers. The vehicle slowed as its guns opened fire, sending blasts of yellow energy into the stunned gangs of Veer-myn sending them diving for cover amidst squeals of pain and shock.

Next the runner pivoted until its guns were pointing towards the Brood Mother and the strange platform, still some way behind the rest of the Veer-myn. It spat a dozen more rays at them both and instantly Stromer felt whatever had a hold on his mind release him.

He gasped as he fell forwards and looked around to see he was not the only marine who had been freed. Beggs and Rains and nearly all of the others were getting back to their feet and picking up their weapons.

Stromer could hear the Brood Mother shrieking in the distance, though whether or not she had been hit by whoever was driving the Veer-myn vehicle he did not know. Its arrival had certainly thrown off whatever or whoever had frozen him and his men though.

The Veer-myn vehicle was still firing as Stromer stood and took stock of the situation.

The Veer-myn front line was in disarray but he guessed the Brood Mother would have them back in line again soon. He looked up to see two of the Terrors were already moving towards the monowheel, firing their cannons at the rogue vehicle.

As for his own forces, nearly half his soldiers, the mob that had followed him from the medblock were still standing. It was not a lot, but it would have to do.

Something exploded up ahead of him and Stromer looked up to see the Veer-myn wheel listing over to one side. Thick smoke was pouring out its central engine block.

It had been hit by one of the Terrors, the giant Veer-myn beasts with heavy guns on their backs. The creature leered at its defeated enemy, its long tongue hanging from its mouth.

The wheel rolled around, tilting over and crashing down to one side. As it fell, its cannons fired one last blast of energy at the Terror that had killed it. A single beam struck the alien monster square between the eyes, killing it in an instant.

Stromer called out over his shoulder.

"Beggs! Rains! On me!"

He didn't know who had been driving the Veer-myn vehicle but he was certain they would need help escaping its burning hulk. He could see movement through the smoke spilling out of the engine block – someone was still alive within it. But even as he started running towards the wrecked vehicle Stromer could also see a gang of Stalkers skittering towards it from the far side.

King yelled out in pain as the heavy gauntlet clamped down on his wrist and pulled. Roca did not stop, but kept on lifting King's entire weight up and out of the overturned tunnel runner.

"Can you stand?" he said as he lowered King down to the ground again. They were outside the camp's perimeter wall and the dirt was packed hard and cold.

King nodded. The pain was coming from his ribs and he was sure he had broken at least two of them when the Terror's gun had hit them.

"Good. Then you can fight." Roca said. He reached back

down into the well of the runner and pulled King's rifle out from where it had been stowed behind the driver's seat. Then he pulled his own rifle clear. It was dark but King could hear the hissing of Veer-myn approaching them from somewhere on the other side of the wheel.

Roca had been right back in the Gorgon lab – King hadn't liked his method of getting them back to the mainland at all. The idea of riding in a Veer-myn vehicle all the way back was bad enough – the machine looked like it might fall apart at any moment and he didn't put much stock in Roca's assurance it was mechanically sound. But being asked to ride pillion, perched behind Roca on top of their bundled weapons and clinging on to his shoulders, was an even less attractive mode of travel. He couldn't argue with Roca's assessment of the situation though – a Veer-myn attack on the marine base was highly likely and could not be allowed to succeed, particularly now they were in possession of the bio-agent Markham had been working on. Roca had refused to tell him exactly what it was but King had figured he didn't need a name. He had seen the hideous malformed things Markham had kept in her lab and he couldn't let whatever did that to a human being get loose. Speed was of the essence and, although even King was not sure exactly how far they were from the mainland, they knew the Veer-myn had a head-start on them.

Reluctantly then, King had climbed aboard.

Even over the noise of the runner's engine, they had both heard the cleaner device go off in the labs behind them as they were rolling out of the canteen. King didn't dare look back for fear of over-balancing the machine, but he could imagine the wave of fire tearing through the place, immolating everything and everyone in there.

Markham was gone as was most of the evidence of her work. All that was left of it was the datapad Roca had secured in a compartment on his armour, and the samples the Veer-myn had stolen.

Roca could worry about tracking down the rest of the Gorgon conspirators. King just wanted to make sure the stolen bio-agent was not released.

Suddenly, the Veer-myn were on top of them.

King heard a low growl from somewhere above him and he looked up to see a Stalker crouched atop the edge of the wheel's armoured track. It sprang down towards him, a long dagger held in each hand, and screeched a Veer-myn battlecry.

Acting as much on instinct as training, King fell backwards awkwardly as he tried to get away from his attacker. He landed painfully on his backside, the packed dirt ground jarring his spine, but he managed to get his rifle up and squeeze off a brace of shots. The Stalker was dead before it hit the ground, half of its bulk landing across King's legs. King yelled out in pain again as he felt something twist unnaturally in one knee.

But there was no time to recover or assess the injury. A dozen more Veer-myn were crowding around on either side of the wheel and over it too.

King dropped one with a blast from his rifle and narrowly dodged a shot from another. He was trapped under the weight of the dead Stalker though, and the next ray struck him on the left shoulder. The arm below it instantly went dead and, terrified it had been blown off, King risked a glance down. The armour plate over his shoulder was sizzling, thin smoke rising off a scorched hole in the armourweave, but it was still at least partially intact. His arm was numb, but it was still there.

He was trapped and wounded, but he was alive. He was also not alone.

King had seen a few good fighters before. He had spent most of his life in one military or another so he had known a lot of professional killers, brawlers, and assassins. Men and women some might even consider 'gifted' in the art of war. Roca was something else.

As soon as the Veer-myn had appeared, he had laid down his rifle and drawn his pistol and a short blue blade, glowing with energy, had slid from a concealed housing on his left wrist. Without hesitation or battlecry he then immediately stepped towards the nearest creature as it ran around one side of the wheel, neatly decapitating it with a shot from the pistol before gutting another Stalker with the blade.

He moved with a calmness that was cold and impassive in its efficiency, but when he struck he did so with a brutality that was breath-taking. A Stalker dropped squealing to the ground, blood fountaining from numerous puncture wounds across its torso, its limbs made useless by precise cuts to tendons and ligaments. Another was dead before it hit the packed earth outside the marine base, its spinal cord severed by a swift slice across the back of its neck, its eyes staring in lifeless shock. Two more Veer-myn tried to grapple with Roca together, each one leaping at him from a different side. Roca simply caught one by the throat in mid-air, twisting its neck with a sharp crack even as he dropped to one knee and turned. The second alien was caught off balance by the sudden violent movement and ploughed into Roca's shoulder, driving the wind from its own lungs. A split-second later and Roca was shooting it through the back of its skull and instantly moving on to his next victim.

Even when rays fired from Veer-myn pistols struck his armour it did not stop or even slow him down. It was as if he knew the shots were coming, had accepted it, trusted that his armour would protect him and incorporated the hits into his battle plan. He did not rush, he did not speak, and he showed no fear. He simply killed and killed again as if nothing could stop him executing every single Veer-myn on Acreon.

Soon, King found himself being practically ignored as the dwindling number of Veer-myn attackers concentrated their attacks on what was clearly the biggest threat to their lives. He was able to finally throw off the dead weight laid out across his legs and struggle back to his feet. A strangled squawk told him Roca had killed the last of the Stalkers, crushing its windpipe with one hand before throwing the Veer-myn aside. If there were any more nearby, they had decided not to continue the attack. All that was left of the ones that had come after them was a dozen corpses.

"Now what?" King said. His arm was still numb, and his right knee felt like he had damaged a tendon.

Roca did not seem to care about his pain though.

"Now we finish this."

His wristblade retracted into its housing and Roca swapped his pistol for the rifle once more. Then he clambered back up onto the side of the overturned wheel.

King was about to ask him what he meant, how he was going to end a war with one weapon, when he heard the sound of footsteps approaching through the darkness at their backs.

He turned as quickly as he could with a damaged knee and brought his weapon up one-handed. Instead of more

Veer-myn though, he saw familiar faces.

"Woah! Don't shoot! King! Is that you? Man, we thought you were dead!"

King lowered his weapon as relief, both at not having to fight again and at seeing old friends, washed over him.

"Stromer? Beggs? Is that Rains?"

There were five of them in total, but although he recognised the other two faces as marines from Sword he couldn't remember their names. All of them looked worn out. Most of the lower half of Stromer's face was covered in dried blood.

"Is this your new team? What the hell happened to you?" King said.

Stromer shook his head as Beggs moved towards the wheel and took a lookout position.

"Yeah, kinda. Things are a little bit chaotic right now. Where have you been?" Stromer said.

King didn't know where to start. He didn't even know what he could tell his team mates of what he had seen and heard during his journey with Roca. He turned to see what the Enforcer was doing, to see if he needed help. But Roca was not moving.

The Enforcer had climbed on top of the tunnel runner and seemed to have been in the act of bringing his rifle to his shoulder. But he had stopped halfway, his weapon still un-aimed, and was as still as a statue atop the commandeered vehicle. No, King realised, not entirely still.

He could hear the small servos in the Enforcer armour whining urgently as if something were stuck or being forced into inaction. He could see the muscles in Roca's jaw working too, as if he was clenching his teeth down on something hard.

"Roca." King said. "Roca – what's happening?"

"Top!" King and Stromer both turned at the hoarse whisper. It was Beggs. "We've got incoming. Looks like maybe twenty 'crawlers. That other Terror is coming too. If we're going to go, we'd better go now."

Stromer looked at King. There were six of them now, and one paralysed Enforcer. If the marines ran, Stromer figured they could probably make it back to the wall. If they ran.

"So," he said. "What do we do?"

CHAPTER 20

The sensors in Roca's armour had alerted him to its presence almost as soon as he had reached the gap in the marine compound's wall and he had seen the evidence of its attack on the frozen and dead marines all around him. He had driven back the frontline of the Veer-myn, but his priority, his very reason for being on Acreon, was to attempt to secure one of the highest value targets in the whole of the GCPS – a live Veer-myn Tangle.

He had climbed atop the tunnel runner intending to scope out its defences, to see how many Veer-myn he would have to kill to isolate the Tangle. But it had sensed him too and it had struck first. Now, Roca's mind was being torn apart.

He could feel the Tangle working its way into his head, four tiny fingers, one for each of its own conjoined skulls, worming their way across the folds of his brain, finding ways into it, exploring it and pushing ever inwards.

He wanted to scream, but could not. It was taking every ounce of his strength and concentration just to resist what the alien monstrosity was doing to him, to stop it from taking him over entirely. He was locked in place, every muscle tense, every servo-motor in his armour straining to resist the muscle spasms that were threatening to tear him apart.

It was painful, in the basic physical sense, but physical pain was something he was built to cope with and resist. What the Tangle was doing, or trying to do to him, went far deeper than that.

As it pried apart the layers of his grey matter, leafing through the folds of his mind with tiny but irresistible and sharp probes, Roca felt himself being divided in two, into a physical and a psychic presence. It was like he could see in two directions at once, like he had two sets of eyes.

In one view he could see the Tangle in the distance in front of him, the Maligni gathered around it, the Mother screeching orders at her children. He was aware of the cool temperature of the night air, could hear the distant sounds of battle still going on, could smell blood. From somewhere behind him he could hear King moving towards him, hear him talking to someone else nearby. He could hear and see marines, some of them those he had evacuated from Almar Square, firing their weapons at approaching Veer-myn. He could feel his own body shaking.

In his mind's eye, he was somewhere else though, in many places in fact, and all at the same time. His psychic self was on the move, following the tendrils of the Tangle as they dived through his subconscious, throwing up scraps of memory, fragments of recall discarded behind them as it moved deeper and deeper.

It was rummaging through those memories, like a burglar ransacking a filing cabinet, checking each one momentarily before dropping it and moving on. Was it looking for something specific? He couldn't tell. But as the Tangle's psychic presence continued to descend through his subconscious Roca began to experience those memories himself. He felt like a small boat being towed in the wake of a much larger vessel and as they travelled he felt every single memory as if he were there in the moment once more, a lifetime experienced in nano-seconds.

He saw things he had forgotten; his childhood, the planet of his birth with its suns and moons and the sea. He felt the warmth of its summers, the chill of its winters. He saw his parents too, their smiling faces. Birthdays, school, academic and physical successes. But then he hit another memory fragment and all the positivity of his early years was replaced with – sadness. It took him a moment to recognise the emotion, but the memory felt raw and real. It was the day he announced he was leaving his family to join the corps. He saw his father's disapproving face, his mother's tears. He experienced the anger of the old man. His rejection.

He saw his induction. The ship that had carried him away from his home, never to see it again. The surgeons, the doctors, the psychoactive specialists. The process of his entire body being stripped down and rebuilt, his nerve fibres replaced, his muscles and internal organs reduced and reconstituted, made better and stronger and faster.

Pain he hadn't even been aware of feeling, things that he thought he had slept through, he relived in an instant.

There were fragments of his career after the program too – the many battles and wars he had fought while enforcing the will of the Council, the hundreds of enemies he had slain in their name. Then it took him to more recent memories. Receiving reports of raised levels of activity in the Euxine and neighbouring sectors. Ships disappearing mid-slide. Colonies going dark. Wars breaking out on frontier planets amidst reports of mysterious diseases and Veer-myn uprisings. The theories at ETCU of links between all these events.

The Tangle saw him drawing up his mission to come to Acreon, choosing Staker and Mouse to help him and then the weeks of surveillance as they tried to track down the Tangle itself. They had tried to flush it out by exterminating the leaders of its nest, identifying its Maligni one by one, particularly the Progenitors, and then terminating them.

Their plan had worked – the Tangle was out in the open now, along with nearly all its nest. But it was Roca that had been caught.

It wasn't finished with his memories either. He saw the Gorgon, the symbol that had been in the hidden laboratory, and relived his conversation with Markham. Heard her suggesting to him once more that someone on the Council, the Council to which he owed all his loyalty, was playing a part in her project.

The Tangle saw his doubts and his suspicions, the inner conflict that had dogged him all the way back through the long dark tunnels to the mainland. He was trained, programmed, to believe in the Council with absolute faith and fidelity. To be completely assured that their will was inviolable and that part of this will was that the Plague must be destroyed without hesitation and at all costs. But if what Markham was suggesting was true...

Roca could feel his mind wandering, the doubt and confusion that Markham had planted in him being exploited and magnified by the alien presence in his head. He knew he would have to deal with the information he had obtained on this damned planet at some point. But for now, he needed to fight.

He began to push back against the Tangle.

The corps and the Council had taken things from him. He knew that and knew he had made sacrifices most men would not believe possible. But he also knew that he had chosen to make them. There were things in the galaxy that had to be destroyed, dangers that would destroy all of mankind, everything the GCPS had built and incorporated if they were not stopped. For every opportunity in the galaxy, there was a threat. The corps had turned him into a weapon, but he was a willing one.

He saw the Tangle's plan now and he focused his mind, driving out the emotions it was using to weaken him and stop him doing his duty. He repeated to himself a mantra he had learned when he first became an Enforcer, so many years ago.

I am a weapon, he said silently, *I am a product of the greatest military program in the history of* mankind.

He turned his psychic self into something hard, a blade of light, an axe, a sword, something to hack and slash and hurt with. He was no longer following the Tangle, a hostage to its intent, but hostile to it. He struck back at the four tendrils probing at his brain and felt its screams of pain as he lashed out.

I am a weapon, he repeated again, *I have no equal and I have no fear.*

It was working. The training, the program, the conditioning. It drove out all doubt and all unnecessary thought. Allowed him to concentrate only on the moment, the here and now. He slashed at the Tangle again and again and felt its panic. It tried to cling onto him but he would not let it. He was not hatred or fury, but pure, cold resolve. This weak alien thing could not resist him.

In his first eye, in the physical world, he could see its physical form in the distance, each one of its ghastly disfigured heads held still and its four noses pointed directly at him as it tried to push his mind back. Its attendant Maligni were hopping and skittering around it as if they could sense its distress but were helpless to intervene. In his mind's eye, the tendrils had become Veer-myn heads too, luminescent things, glowing red with anger and frustration and now more than a little fear.

I am a weapon, he told them, *I have no room for emotion, I exist only to do their will!*

He struck out again and again and this time he knew he had broken the Veer-myn's will. He forced it back up and out of the deepest recesses of his mind.

His physical self could feel sweat was running down his face as he fought the alien into submission. But he did not stop there. He kept on pushing, using the very same psychic connection the Tangle had created as a bridge into *its* mind-space.

I am the will of the Council, he told himself, told *it. I am nobody's toy!*

The Tangle shrank back before him, its psychic presence not entirely defeated and yet knowing it had met something very close to its match. For a second Roca felt what it felt, saw how it could sense every living thing on the battlefield, human and Veer-myn alike. Its power was impressive.

Around his physical form Roca could hear the marines that had come to aid him and King, fighting for their lives. They could have abandoned him when the Tangle attacked but they had not. They had stood and fought to defend him.

They would need his help. He would need to be quick.

Tell me who you are, Roca thought at the creature in front

of him. *Tell me where you came from.*
Tell me why this *world.*

Something had changed. Oneyul felt it, as if heavy chains
had been lifted from her shoulders. The Veer-myn thing's
hold on her was gone. It had been holding her still, but
then she had felt it drift away, as it its attention had been
pulled elsewhere. She didn't care where it had gone, she was
just glad to be free of it.

Her eyes were watering and she wiped blood away from
beneath her nose. Beside her, Vallow was coming to and
she could hear more of the injured on the rooftop behind
them recovering as well.

"What happened?" Vallow said. He had fallen on his arm
when he passed out and he winced as he lifted himself
back up.

Oneyul leaned down and picked up her rifle. She could
see flashes of laser fire out by the breach.

"Not sure I know," she said. "It doesn't matter though.
It's time to finish it." she said.

She lifted the rifle up and braced it across the railing,
aiming it towards the Veer-myn positions.

The 'crawlers were scattered. Many of them were dead
and the rest were falling back from the marines who had
survived their attack. Even the Terrors seemed to have been
all cut down.

They weren't what she was looking for though. She
panned across the battlefield until she found the thing that
had tormented her and her friends. Even though its mental
fingers had been removed from her head, it still took some
effort to make herself focus in on the infant Veer-myn on
its platform. There were other Veer-myn with it, Maligni

by the looks of them, but she could see it nonetheless. Its four heads were no longer outstretched towards the marines though. Now all four were pointed to something on her right. She followed their eyeless gaze and found the Enforcer, the one that had taken King with him, kneeling atop the overturned wreck of the vehicle she had seen him drive out of the tunnel in.

He was quite still though, his weapon not quite raised to a firing position, and she knew immediately why.

She sighted in again on the Veer-myn on the platform. Her targeting reticule lit up as she focused in on one of its tiny heads.

The Maligni were moving around it and she had to wait for a clean shot, knowing she might only get one chance to do what she need to do.

She forced herself to relax, to not let adrenaline make her twitch, or anything else on the battlefield distract her.

Her moment came and she exhaled slowly as she squeezed the trigger.

CHAPTER 21

Roca felt the shock of it as the energy beam penetrated the cortex of one of its minds. It was as if all the light in the universe disappeared at once. It was like waking up from a dream where you had seen wonders to find oneself blind. The loss of perception, of sensation, was astounding, so much so it took him a moment to realise he was no longer seeing through the Tangle's eyes, but only his own.

He had only been linked with it for a few moments, but he was reminded of how it had felt to become an Enforcer, how much powerful his senses were at the end of the program than his natural pure-gene ones had ever been.

Normal sounds began to flood back into his brain as he readjusted, normal sights to his eyes.

He was still on top of the tunnel runner, still holding his rifle in his hands.

Beneath him and around him, the Drakenhof marines were still firing their weapons and shouting. Laser light was still flashing sporadically across the battlefield and there were dozens of dead Veer-myn around them. Several dead humans lay amongst them too. But the marines were cheering and as he looked around himself, he saw why.

The Veer-myn were running.

He felt dizzy, a feeling he had not felt for many years.

Suddenly he was falling, tumbling sideways over the edge of the wheel as the dizziness momentarily overwhelmed him. He crashed to the ground, barely able to brace himself for the fall or stretch out a hand to stop himself.

He lay on his back, looking up at a cloudy night's sky. He could feel his conditioning kicking in, fighting to steady him and help him recover from the disorientation of the violent disconnect he had just experienced.

A familiar face appeared in his eyeline.

"King?"

"Yes, Roca," the face said. "Are you alright?"

It took two of them to haul him up to his feet, King and the marine called Stromer.

"I don't know what you did up there," Stromer said, "but it worked. We won! They're running away!"

He was right. The Veer-myn were panicking, retreating away from the base as fast as they could. Here and there a few were still firing back towards the marines pursuing them, but there was no real steel to it. They were disorganised, mere stragglers. The main body of their force was utterly routed and rapidly disappearing into the darkness, presumably heading back to their tunnels.

The loss of the Tangle had affected them somehow. Roca knew it was able to control them, at least partially. But was its loss more than a tactical one? Could it also have been acting as a kind of talisman for them too?

It was all tactically valuable information and he knew the analysts at the corps and ETCU would be grateful for it. It meant little to Roca though.

He stooped down and picked up his rifle, then aimed it towards the retreating Veer-myn. It was too late though. Of the Brood Mother and her tangled offspring there was no sign.

He cursed quietly.

"I didn't do anything." Roca said.

Stromer had left them, gone to help deal with some of the wounded marines, and Roca was alone with King.

He looked down at the marine.

"You didn't run." he said.

It was a question as much as it was a statement and King nodded his answer.

"Well, I told you I might surprise you one day." he said.

"Yes, you did." Roca said. "But you didn't run when you could have. If you did, I would probably be dead."

"Yeah, well," King said, "I think we both know there are worse things than you in the galaxy now."

Roca conceded the point.

"But it's all over now." King said. "I mean, this isn't another trap, is it? We follow them and they ambush us again?"

"No," said Roca, "It's not a trap. They're beaten and they're running. They lost something very important tonight and their will to fight went with it."

King nodded. "Good. So it's done then."

Roca turned back towards the breach in the wall and the camp buildings beyond it.

"Not quite," he said, "There's one more to do deal with."

King turned too and followed Roca's gaze. He swore as he realised what Roca was saying.

"So it wasn't here then?" he said. "Ok, let's go."

Roca put a hand out on the marine's shoulder, stopping

him from marching towards the camp.

"No." Roca said. "Not this time. This is something I need to do alone."

King turned and looked defiantly at the Enforcer.

"Now you want to leave me behind? After dragging me halfway to hell and back? And after I saved your life?"

Roca's face was stern but he spoke calmly.

"I do." he said. "Corporal, you are wounded. I am not leaving you here because I don't value you, but because I can do this better alone. Stay here. Stay with your comrades. Get some medical attention."

King stared at Roca for a moment. He wanted argue with him more but he had to admit he really did not feel like chasing after him into more danger. His ribs were sore and his leg was starting to really hurt too. He looked around to make sure no one was close enough to hear him.

"Ok. Fine. But you swear you'll take care of 'it', though, right? You won't let it get out."

"You have my word." Roca said. "I'll die before I let that happen."

Roca shouldered his rifle and started to walk towards the camp. Then he stopped and turned back to face the watching King again.

"Corporal King, your service has been noted. You have the Council's thanks."

Then he was gone, disappearing into the darkness and through the breach.

King watched him go.

"Council be damned." he said.

Roca jumped up and engaged his jetpack, letting it push him up and onto the roof of the building ahead of him. He knew he didn't have far to travel and the main Veer-myn force had been routed. There might still be a few stragglers left in the base though, and he could not afford to be slowed down.

Many Veer-myn had infiltrated the camp, either through the breach in the wall or when the tunnellers had arrived. Roca suspected those weren't the only ways they had to get in. But there was only one Veer-myn he needed to deal with now. He had seen it through the Tangle's psychic sight when he and it had been locked together in their mental battle. It was a single Malignus, the same one that had infiltrated the Gorgon laboratory and discovered the secret bioweapons program. The Tangle had never 'seen' this Malignus with its own eyes, so Roca did not know what it would look like either. But he knew where it was going.

During the journey along the tunnels back to the mainland, he had assumed it would be with the rest of the Veer-myn assaulting the camp. He did not know enough about Veer-myn technology to be sure, but he thought it likely their Maligni would incorporate the samples into their chemical weaponry somehow. That had not been the case. He had learned from the Tangle the Veer-myn plan was much simpler than that.

The assault at the wall, even the tunnellers and Stalker infiltration were a diversion, attacks all meant to draw Drakenhof's strength away from the Veer-myn's true target.

Roca stopped running and crouched down. He had scaled to the top of a two-storey administration building and he was approaching the edge of its roof. Some thirty metres ahead of him was the Veer-myn's target building. He pulled his rifle from his shoulder and switched its sights to night-vision.

The monochromatic shape of fortified Shensig tiles filled the sight's screen as he panned across the front of the base's armoury. Within it was the expeditionary force's entire stock of weaponry, ammunition, and high explosives. He had bent the Tangle to his own will, forcing it back in on itself until it had showed him its nest's plan: a massive explosion. A detonation within the armoury, kickstarted by an explosive device the Malignus was carrying, laced with the bio-agent it had stolen from Gorgon.

Biological warfare was not something the Enforcer Corps typically employed. But, they were trained to deal with it anyway and Roca knew this was how he would quickly disperse a bio-agent if he had to. He could already feel desert air whipping around him – the winds coming in off the sea would quickly carry the bio-agent halfway around Acreon if it was let loose.

The tankers containing the camp's supply of incendiary gel were still parked across the road from the armoury and movement near them caught his eye. His armour's sensors registered a target. Clouds passing overhead meant there was almost no natural light but in the infrared glow of his scope he could see it skitter through the shadows towards the base of the armoury wall. He adjusted the focus, zooming in on the huddled form as it stopped in a corner between a thick reinforced stanchion and an armoured Shensig plate.

Huddled in the darkness was a lone Veer-myn. It was only lightly armoured, he saw, presumably to help it infiltrate the camp without being detected, and it was carrying a heavy-looking bag at its hip, hung on a broad strap that ran across its shoulder. Roca could not see through the material, but it seemed about the right size for a small explosive device. He had to be sure though. If he fired and revealed himself and then found it was not the right Veer-myn he might not get another chance. His real target would likely be spooked and either find another way to detonate its device or simply disappear, taking the Gorgon sample with it.

The Veer-myn in his sights only had one ear, the other one worn or chewed down to a stub. The amplified light being collected by his scope flared brightly as the Veer-myn glanced behind itself quickly. It had some kind of electronic device in place of one of its eyes too. Recognition struck Roca immediately – he had seen this creature before. Almar Square – this had been one of the Maligni attending the Progenitor he and his team had terminated. Somehow it had escaped the onslaught of the Accuser and now it was here.

It had to be the one.

The Malignus turned back to the armoury and Roca could see it looking up towards the building's roof. He flicked his vision upwards for a second and saw there was a heavy air vent, its slatted cover visible near the top of the wall, roughly three metres from the ground. The Malignus' haunches quivered as it crouched and prepared to try to leap for the vent. Somehow it planned to force its way in through the vent and, once inside, into the armoury itself.

Before it could jump, Roca squeezed the trigger on his rifle.

It was a precision shot and the Malignus span round as the beam hit it in the back of its left shoulder. A chunk of its armour flew away and bounced off the armoury wall. The wounded Veer-myn dropped forwards to its knees.

Roca jumped down from his firing position, his jetpack slowing his descent. He left his rifle on the roof and when he landed he instead drew his pistol. The Veer-myn was still alive and it looked up at it him with a mix of hatred and disbelief written across its face. It was breathing heavily and blood was pouring from the exit wound on its shoulder, but it was not done. Suddenly it pulled its own pistol from a holster on its belt and Roca had to dodge to one side as a stream of yellow rays poured towards him. The Veer-myn rose on unsteady legs and turned back towards the armoury, looking up again at the distant vent cover, still intent on carrying out the mission its Mother had given it.

Roca could admire its devotion to its mission, its determination to fulfil it no matter the cost. But he could not allow it to succeed. He strode forwards, aiming his pistol carefully at the creature's head and fired again and again. The Malignus dropped down for the final time.

Its blood was forming a pool on the ground beneath it as Roca stood over it. He remained still for a moment, his weapon still sighted on the corpse.

The cover on the Malignus' bag had fallen partly open and Roca carefully lifted it some more with the barrel of his weapon. He could see a metallic device within it, a bundle of wires and circuitry. There were a few distinct components though – he recognised a military-grade fuse cap, a miner's timer. It was a bomb.

The clouds broke through overhead then and moonlight glinted off glass. There were six small vials attached to the Malignus' device, each filled with a pale green liquid. Crucially, none of them appeared to be broken.

Gorgon had not been his reason for coming to Acreon. But the Tangle was dead and he knew this was more important. Whoever had brought the bio-agent here would need to be found. But first he had to take care of the agent itself.

Roca kneeled down and was about to extend his wristblade

in order to cut the bag free from the Veer-myn corpse when light exploded from behind him. A dozen blasts of energy struck him almost instantaneously, overwhelming his armour and sending him crashing to the ground.

His suit's systems screamed electronic warnings into his ear as he fell. He ignored them and rolled to one side as he tried to bring his pistol to bear. He felt no pain, but his arm was slow, the muscles damaged by the shots he had taken.

Another blast of energy immediately struck him on the hand and sent his shattered pistol flying from his grip. He grunted with effort as he tried to push himself away from his assailant but he was stopped when he felt the wall of the armoury at his back.

The sensor package on the side of his helmet had been damaged and he could hear it sparking uselessly. All he had was his enhanced senses.

Beside one of the parked tankers stood a single figure, obscured by shadow but holding a heavy laser rifle at its hip.

Roca's armour was still sending him warning messages as he focused in on the man who had shot him.

"So," he said, "it's you. You were Markham's contact here."

The figure stepped forward, its weapon still trained on Roca.

"Yes," said Major Corrick. "I was."

CHAPTER 22

"Do you have the samples, Lieutenant?"

Roca resisted the temptation to look towards the dead Veer-myn lying beside him. He knew now what it was that Corrick wanted and he had a good idea that not having it was all that was keeping him alive.

Roca was already badly hurt – several bones in his right hand had been fractured by Corrick's last shot and his suit was recording bleeding from wounds around his shoulders and back and internally around some of his organs. The suit was delivering a mix of painkillers, healing agents, and anti-infection drugs but it was damaged too. Repair systems were struggling to restore damaged fibre bundles and get him back to his feet. It was telling him the best he could hope for was fifty percent combat effectiveness and only then if he could give it enough time.

"Samples? What samples?" he said.

Corrick scowled. He took a few steps forward, moving out of the shadows around the tanker. He moved cautiously, his eyes checking the rooftops of the buildings around him, alert for any lurking Veer-myn that might be nearby. He kept the barrel of his weapon aimed towards Roca at all times.

"You know what samples," he said. "The samples this alien scum stole and which you came back here to retrieve."

He stopped a few metres away from Roca and nodded towards the dead Malignus.

"These things have caused me no end of trouble," he said. "When I saw them on the surveillance feeds from our little project here on Acreon, well, I thought it was all over. But it turns out they were not the only unwanted visitors, were they?

"By the way, I assume we all have you to thank for our not being flattened by the Hilton when it came down?"

Roca nodded but he grunted with discomfort. He could feel the small bones in his hand reknitting. His armour was working in conjunction with the chemical agents in his system, adding tension to help the bones reform. Something shifted inside him as one of his organs, what he had in place of a liver, went through a similar process.

"Yes. The ship was a trap. It was set up to hit this place as almost as soon as anyone stepped aboard it."

Corrick hesitated.

"Really? A trap? That is – unexpected."

Roca nodded.

"It would appear we are not the only ones who know about you, about Gorgon." he said.

Corrick's gaze drifted for a second as if he was lost in thought, though he still kept his weapon levelled at Roca. Then his eyes snapped back to the Enforcer.

"Maybe. But what *do* you know, Lieutenant? Very, very little, I think. You stumbled upon our facility here, despite my best efforts to put you safely out of the way. I watched your conversation with the late Doctor Markham – there was only one way for her to contact me, but I could always see her – and you may have an idea what she was doing, but no proof. And I doubt you have had the opportunity to tell anyone else about it either. You certainly couldn't have exposed me yet.

Roca's armour was reporting it had nearly finished repairs to some of his secondary systems. It was also registering a drop in blood pressure that it was compensating for but would require serious attention soon. He had to keep Corrick talking.

"I know about the Council. You're not the first agent of Gorgon I have found." he said.

Corrick raised an eyebrow at that.

"The Council?" he said. He seemed to consider Roca's words for a moment.

"No," he said slowly. "No, I don't think I believe you. They may make you experts in many forms of combat, but your bluffing is quite amateur. I think if you knew even a fraction of how deep the Gorgon has penetrated, well, as our good commandant said, you would not be here alone."

"Patrin?" Roca said.

"Yes," Corrick said. He had stepped closer now, close enough to see the dead Malignus beside Roca more clearly. "The commandant is ignorant about many things, including how many men and resources I have been able to funnel to my true masters using his authority codes. But he does not underestimate your corps' destructive power and neither do I."

Corrick leaned forward slightly, still just out of Roca's reach, and a broad smile broke across his face.

"Ah," he said. "Is that some kind of explosive device in

its bag? That's it, isn't it? It was going to use that to spread the bio-agent. Which means the samples are still there too, which means I no longer need you."

Corrick stood up straight and lifted his rifle to one shoulder.

"Who could have guessed it would be you, an Enforcer of all things that would save me from utter disaster? Well, we work with what we have. You have my thanks."

Roca braced himself. His armour was close to ready but its power reserves were low. It would have to be enough. Before he could make his move, another voice echoed from the wall behind him.

"Don't do it, Corrick! Drop your weapon!"

The voice came from near where Roca had shot the Malignus, from someone at ground level. Corrick turned on the spot and fired immediately, sending a brace of high-powered shots into the darkness. At least one of them hit its mark and Roca heard someone cry out in pain.

Before Corrick could fire again though, Roca ignited his jetpack, using the last of the energy his armour had been able to supply it to push himself up and forward. The jets sputtered as they flared with white light and his bulk smashed into Corrick's back.

The Major cried out in surprise as the Enforcer drove into him, throwing him to the ground. The rifle flew out of his grip as Corrick tried to buck Roca loose and Roca felt some of the recently repaired fingers in his hand strain to stay whole. Corrick twisted, driving an elbow back and into Roca's jaw and the Enforcer felt a tooth shatter as the blow connected. Blood pressure warnings flashed in his helmet's visor again and for a moment he lost sight of his opponent.

Then Corrick was on him. For an un-enhanced human,

he was surprisingly quick and strong. He lashed out with a booted foot, striking Roca in the chest and pushing him back again into the armoury. Roca found his focus and determination were admirable, almost Enforcer-like. But the look of hatred on his face as he pulled a heavy knife from its sheath on his shoulder was purely human. The major leaped forward, the blade flashing in the moonlight, murder in his eyes.

As quick as he was though, and as wounded as Roca was, the Enforcer was still quicker.

Corrick's charge was suddenly halted and he let out a surprised gasp. His blade was still held high above him, poised to strike, but all his strength had left him. The knife slowly fell from his fingers and harmlessly to the ground as Corrick looked down at his chest. He was impaled on Roca's wristblade, the glowing blue tip protruding from his back.

The monomolecular edge had cut through his armour-weave chestplate with ease but it had been Corrick's own momentum that had caused it to penetrate him so deeply. Roca, with the strength he still had, carefully eased the major down, withdrawing the blade with a wet sucking noise from the dying man's chestplate.

He turned towards the shadows where Corrick had fired his weapon.

"Corporal King," he said, "are you still alive?"

King shuffled forwards, leaning heavily on the rifle he was now using as a kind of walking stick. His leg had been bound in a hasty field dressing and he clutched a fresh wound in one arm with the other hand.

"Yeah," he said, "still alive."

"Good," said Roca. "I believe I gave you an order to stay where you were."

"Yeah, well," King hobbled over towards where Corrick lay, "I never completely agreed to following your orders."

King looked down at Corrick. He was still alive though clearly in great pain. He clutched at his wrist with his hand while his mouth worked almost soundlessly as he looked up at the stars. His eyes met King's then and there was a moment of recognition.

Corrick's lips were wet with blood. "Corporal King," he said, "I'm glad to see you here."

King slowly kneeled down beside him, taking care not to further strain his knee.

"Really?" he said. "Doesn't look like me being here's worked out too well for you."

Corrick closed his eyes.

"You'd be surprised," he said. "We all serve as we can. But I am surprised at your choice."

King looked confused.

"Choice? What choice?"

Corrick turned his head to one side and spat out a wad of blood. He glared at Roca standing nearby.

"You made a choice, whether you know it or not." he said through bloodstained teeth. He looked back at King. "But if you survive what comes next, there's one thing you should do. You should ask your new friend here about his past. About what he was before they made him a 'Forward Observer'. Ask him about his time fighting rogue corporations in the Persid sector."

King recoiled from the major.

"He – what? Wait. What do you mean 'what comes next'? What have you done?"

Corrick was not just smiling now. At first King thought he was going into shock, his body trembling as his lifeblood

soaked into the ground beneath him. But then King realised the major was actually laughing.

He was still clutching at his wrist with one hand and
Roca leaned down to pull his hand loose. Beneath it was a
glowing command unit, flashing confirmation of a delivered order.

"What little you have learned of Gorgon will die with you
here. The Genoa is in orbit directly above us. I just sent it
a kill code for this location." Corrick said.

Roca stood up, the damaged servos in his armour whirring as he looked up at the cloudy sky above Sword Base.

"Roca," King said, "What did he say? What did he do?"

Something flashed high above the cloud cover. It seemed
like lightning but King hadn't felt any storm approaching.
He understood why almost immediately.

A massive beam of plasma lanced down through the
clouds, striking the ground somewhere on the far side of
the ATC tower. King and Roca heard something exploding under the impact. The ground shook beneath their feet
but there was more to come.

The first blast was a target-marker, a ranging shot intended
to establish the firing ship had correctly established a solu-
tion. The sky flashed again and again, lighting the base up
like daylight, as the Genoa opened fire in earnest. Dozens
of highly-charged beams streaked down into the compound,
vaporising whatever they struck, sending fragments of buildings, vehicles, Veer-myn and marines flying.

As the world exploded into flames all around them,
Roca looked King in the eye, his face a mask of cold
determination.

"Run." he said.

EPILOGUE I

The wall of screens in Commandant Patrin's office quarters painted a picture of a city and a world that was recovering and was well on its way to being completely normal once again.

The screens showed a variety of feeds. Video-casts from local sources and a few extra-planetary ones mixed with data streams from the city's various monitoring and AI systems. One screen was showing a news report from the coast where work had begun on several new floating factories. Each of them would harvest blooms of algae off the coast and turn them into foodstuffs for export to worlds further out on the fringe. Another showed a stream of passengers disembarking the latest shuttle to arrive at the Memorial Spaceport. More and more workers were coming back to Acreon every day, according to the subtitles that scrolled across the bottom of the picture. On a third, the sector's most popular sports-talk net was even reporting that a certain well-known corporation back in the Core was considering building a new DreadBall stadium in Guiders City.

It had been nearly two months since the battle of Sword

Base and not a single Veer-myn had been spotted on Acreon since that night. Guiders City, Acreon itself, was not just recovering after its brief scuffle with alien invaders, it was thriving. It was as if the eradication of the Veer-myn had brought a new confidence in the planet and now people with money were taking notice of it.

The man credited with making all this possible stood now, with arms folded, scanning the bank of monitor screens that filled the wall before him with a sense of quiet satisfaction.

The firing of the Genoa's weapons at Sword Base itself was being described in company journals and literature as an act of daring boldness. Officially, the action had not only repelled the Veer-myn in their savage and unprovoked assault on a corporate encampment, it had all but wiped them out. The steel of a man brave enough to order such a thing was not to be doubted. Or so the journals said.

Commandant Marcus Patrin knew there was probably more to the story than that. But as he stood watching the world rebuild itself, he did not care.

Firing the weapons of an orbiting assault cruiser on a company-occupied site was not a typically sanctioned event. The safeguards and security gates around the computers aboard the Genoa, the ones tasked with controlling the firing systems for its plasma cannon, were quite extensive. And yet they had been circumvented by the delivery of recognised and authorised codes.

Patrin knew he had not given the Genoa its kill-codes, no matter what the digital records said.

He *had* ordered the Genoa to make itself ready to act when it achieved orbit above Acreon. It was only prudent, given how deeply the Veer-myn had penetrated the base.

But he had never felt it necessary to actually order the last ditch attempt to eliminate the invaders. It would surely have been overkill.

Someone had sent the codes though and Patrin thought he knew who. There were only so many people that *could* have done it, after all. But Corrick, his prime suspect, had been confirmed to be amongst the dead, one more soldier that had died a hero defending Sword Base. Patrin could live with that. For now, he would keep his suspicions to himself.

The firing of the Genoa's weapons at the compound had not come without cost. He would not deny that. The base itself had been largely levelled by the combination of the Genoa's firepower and the detonation of the thermal gel tankers. One had taken a direct hit from a plasma blast and erupted like a steel volcano, sending flaming gel hundreds of metres into the air before it rained back down on the camp. The medblock and most of the north wall had been reduced to melted rubble and there was very little left of the ATC tower at all. Luckily, at least as far as Patrin was concerned, the Command Bunker had survived practically completely intact. It was the safest place in the compound by design.

The barracks blocks had all been destroyed though, leaving the surviving marines camping outside for the foreseeable future. Not that there were many survivors.

Reinforcements from the Genoa had found numerous marine corpses amongst the smoking ruins of the base and tattered remnants of the Veer-myn invaders. Scattered reports that most of the Veer-myn had in fact been pushed out of the base and engaged on the dusty ground beyond its wall were being treated as unreliable – no senior commander could corroborate them and the marines involved were being advised to keep their fantastic stories to themselves. Patrin expected there would be some awkward questions for him to field from the accountants on Karkorum when his tour on Acreon was done. But he knew as well as they did that results were all that really mattered and the contract on Acreon had been successfully executed by any measure.

Even the rumours the Enforcer, the troublesome Lieutenant Roca, had been seen in Sword Base moments before the Genoa opened fire, did not worry him significantly. He had diverted Roca and his team up to investigate the drifting Hilton at the late Major Corrick's suggestion and had, like everyone else, assumed he was lost when the hauler crashed down into the seas to the east. Whether he had indeed died aboard the ship or, somehow, later within the compound, it did not matter. Patrin could truthfully say he had not interfered with him or his precious Council-given mission either way.

No, he had not sent the kill-codes to the Genoa and he knew there was likely more to the battle than he had been party to. But he was content taking the credit for the outcome. Unofficial word had already come from Karkorum that he should expect a promotion on his return.

Somebody coughed quietly behind Patrin and he turned to find Lieutenant Jay standing by his shoulder.

"Yes, Lieutenant?" Patrin said, still smiling. "Is everything in order?"

Jay coughed again and looked embarrassed.

"Sir," she said, "It's complicated. But you asked to be informed of anything unusual happening."

"Yes. And?"

"Sir, I'm sorry, sir. I'm really not sure how this happened, but, well, we've lost control of some of the orbital tracking sats."

The two were standing in Patrin's private office, a room that adjoined the command centre of the bunker. Over Jay's shoulder, through the open doorway, Patrin could see several of his staff clustered around the workstation designated to receive tracking data from the shipping control satellites orbiting the planet.

The satellites belonged to Almar Inc. and were linked to the NaviCorp system, helping co-ordinate the movement of traffic through the sector. The temporary loss of one was not necessarily catastrophic – ships could still use their inbuilt guidance systems to avoid collisions and even to slide out of the system. But it could make Drakenhof blind to any incoming vessels.

"Oh?" he said. "How many?"

"Well," Jay said. "All of them."

Patrin began walking towards the workstations that were apparently no longer functional. The day had started out so well but he could feel his happiness draining away at the thought of dealing with whatever malfunction had occurred in the satellite network.

"Lost?" he said. Jay hurried along behind him.

"Yes, sir. We're still receiving data, well, some data. But the sats don't seem to respond to our orders anymore."

Patrin stood behind a staff officer, looking down and over his shoulder at the man's screen. It showed lines of code, code Patrin did not understand at all.

"So what are we receiving?" he said.

The officer's fingers flickered over the keys of his holo-keyboard and the display changed. Now Patrin had a better idea of what he was looking at.

"That's the local system registry?" he said. He was looking at a three-dimensional representation of Acreon and its surrounding space. An icon on the planet's surface marked out his own location and several more, moving around in orbit above it, showed ships at anchor. Each one had an ident code. Patrin could even place some of them against notifications he had received that morning of the arrival of transports bearing workers and material from other colonies.

"Yeah, it is." the officer said. "I mean, yes, sir. Only, the data is frozen. It's like the entire NaviCorp system is no longer responding. No one can calculate slide data or – wait. "What in the Core?"

A new glowing red icon had suddenly appeared on the display, very close to the planet and without any alphanumeric ident code. Beside the new arrival, the screen simply read 'Unidentified'.

"What just happened?" Patrin said. "Who is that? How did they get so close without anyone warning us?"

"I – I don't know, sir."

Jay had picked up a large datapad and paired it with the system registry. Now it was showing the same display of the planet's orbit.

"Sir, I can tell you that." she said. "It's some kind of strike-class starship. It is now in orbit directly above us and we didn't see them coming because they didn't use the system slide point. They slid directly into orbit. Straight into the planet's grav-well."

Patrin looked at her in some confusion.

"What? But that makes no sense. Anyone doing that would be in danger of simply being pulled straight into the planet's mass. They would be destroyed. Why would anyone take that risk?" he said.

"Usually we do it because we don't want anyone to know we're coming."

Patrin's head jerked up. Every display in the command centre had changed to one image, a single face. One Patrin had thought he would never see again.

"Lieutenant Roca?" he said.

Roca nodded. He was sitting in a heavily padded seat and from the array of instrument displays around him and the faint background hum it was clear he was aboard the newly orbiting vessel.

"But I – we, we thought you were dead." Patrin said.

"No," Roca said. "Although it was a close thing in the end. But as you can see, I am very much alive."

"Ah," said Patrin. "Very good. And Corporal King, is he with you as well?"

Roca looked thoughtful.

"Corporal King is alive. He is where he needs to be right now."

"Ah." said Patrin. The surprise at seeing Roca again was quickly replaced by irritation. "Very good indeed. But it seems that once again you are disrupting my operation. And once again I do not know why. Perhaps you missed the CorpsNet update, but this planet has been cleared of alien invaders."

Roca smiled.

"No, I read the update and I know all about the Veer-myn. More than you would believe."

"Then may I ask," Patrin said, "why are you here again?"

Roca looked away from the screen for a second and seemed to be saying something to someone off-camera, confirming understanding of something, perhaps. Then he looked back at Patrin.

"Firstly, Commandant Patrin, this planet is no longer a Drakenhof concern. You should consider yourself relieved of all responsibilities in this system. I will give you a full day to pack up your operation and ship out."

"What?" said Patrin. "This is outrageous! I thought we established before that you do not have the –"

Roca had raised a hand, silencing Patrin. He leaned forward until his face filled the screens around the room.

"Do you remember our first meeting, Commandant?" Roca said. "You told me you thought a full-scale strike force of Enforcers would be impressive. Well, what do you think now?"

Alarm tones began to sound at workstations around the command centre. The staff officer sat in front of Patrin swore loudly as his display was suddenly filled with more 'unidentified' glowing red icons.

Patrin swallowed heavily. He turned to Jay who was staring wide-eyed at her datapad.

"Sir, tracking is back online. Nine more ships, same size as the first just slid into orbit. The planet is – surrounded! They've deployed attack ships! We're reading at least forty signals breaking atmosphere now. They're all coming – here!"

Patrin scowled and took the datapad from Jay.

"Pull yourself together, Lieutenant," he said as he looked at the real-time display of ships deploying above him. "If they wanted to kill us we'd already be dead."

He thrust the pad back into Jay's hands and turned to face Roca again.

"Lieutenant, I don't understand this but I want you to know the Drakenhof clan will not stand for it." Patrin said.

"I think you'll find they will," said Roca. "All you need to know is the Council has agreed with my assessment of

the danger on Acreon and it turns out they are very willing to overrule your company's claim to it. This planet
belongs to me now."

Patrin frowned.

"But why? The Veer-myn threat is –"

"The Veer-myn threat is not the real danger to this planet.
Or this system." Roca interrupted.

"Then what is?" Patrin said.

Roca paused.

"I learned many things from my previous mission on
Acreon." he said. "We all assumed that the Veer-myn arriving on the Hilton were some kind of invasion force. But
they were not."

"Then what were they?" Patrin said.

"I have come to believe they were only a first strike." he
said. "A probe. Designed to test our defences maybe. Or
perhaps destroy something important."

Patrin shook his head.

"A first strike?" he said. "A first strike by whom?"

Roca looked grim. He reached out to one side of the seat
he was in and picked up his helmet. He placed it over his
head and Patrin could hear the seals and locks snapping
shut. Roca looked at the camera again.

"By an enemy unlike anything you have ever seen, Commandant. By something far worse than me. You have one
day. Roca out."

He leaned forward again and Patrin's screen went blank.

EPILOGUE II (POST CREDITS SCENE)

It was dark in the Mother's chamber and warm as always. It was unusually quiet though.

The nest was greatly weakened, the brethren having been almost wiped out. Nearly all those that had fled the battle at the humans' camp were hurt in one way or another. But some had survived, made it back to their home, and so would the nest.

Most of the lower caste gangs had retreated to their private lairs, their own parts of the nest's tunnel network where they could lick their wounds and feed. Where they could rest and recover. The gangs that were too small to function usefully any more would be folded into others. There might be squabbles, more deaths even, as the new gangs chose new leaders. But they would go on.

The Maligni had gone to their laboratories and workshops to start rebuilding the nest's defences. Their Terrors had been destroyed and their weapons depleted, but they had new materials to work with and there was always more arriving on the surface. When the time came to fight again they would be ready.

So for now, in her chamber, the Brood Mother was almost completely alone.

As soon as her attendants had stripped off her battered armour, removed her metal carapace and let her flesh roll free again, she had chased them all away, hissing and biting at their rumps as they went. Few dared approach her now as she lay on her bed, hissing and spitting, her tail thumping from side to side. Her eyes were closed, but she could not rest.

The loss of the battle had hurt her deeply. Her children were numerous and nearly every one was replaceable, but she still felt each death like a small wound. The failure of her Malignus' plan was a grave blow to her pride too. But neither it nor the deaths of her children were the source of her greatest pain.

Behind her lay what was left of her strange conjoined litter. Its injury was far worse than anything she had suffered. Its body had been damaged and one of its four heads lay still on its bed, a neat hole bored through its tiny skull like a third blind eye socket. The others were all alive and awake though, and they quivered and trembled, their jaws opening and closing soundlessly.

The Mother and all her children had felt its pain and its confusion when the human shot it. The psychic shock had been so strong the Mother had barely been able to maintain enough discipline to order what was left of her forces back into the safety of the tunnels.

Since then, the only ones she had allowed to remain in her presence were the three Maligni that had guarded the litter since its birth. They moved around it now, muttering and chittering to themselves and each other, arguing about what to do, how best to treat what was left of it and what kind of omen it was that one head had died while the others still lived.

She could not hear them though. She could only hear it.

It no longer only spoke to her in a quiet whisper. Maybe it was because of the wound, or maybe it was a power it had always had, but now her litter could show her things too.

Her eyes were closed, but she saw another world. Somewhere distant and yet reachable on a good starship. A world very different to hers, with masses of green trees and rivers of flowing water. It should have been a place teeming with life but it had become the home of death.

There were monsters there. She saw them, hulking, deformed, full of rage. She could tell many of them had once been human, but something else had got into them, something alien that made them different. It filled them with hunger and rage.

She saw the rage-things hunting. They were moving through the streets and tunnels of cities, passing through the shadows of buildings they had once built themselves. They were hunting. They were hunting her kind, but not to kill. They were stunning the brethren and gassing them. Capturing them.

She knew with certainty then that these captured brethren were the same ones that had landed on her world and sparked the war she had just lost. They had been sent by the rage-things.

Now the Tangle showed her their armies gathering. There were more of them than she knew how to count. Gang after gang of warped humans passed by her sight, long arms grasping weapons wrapped in rags and fragments of skin. Claws and teeth wet with spittle and blood. Overhead the sky was black and lightning raced across it.

She realised then she was not the only one watching the infected. There was another rage-thing, a female like her. She stood in the darkness, watching her armies go by. Controlling them without words. Her eyes glowed like embers and the Mother of the brethren knew that she was *their* mother.

The vision faded away and now the litter began to scream again. On her bed, the Mother rolled and roared as she felt all the litter's pain and suffering once more. And now its fear.

The litter screamed the same thing into her head again and again and again until she screamed with it.

"They are coming!" the litter screamed. "They are coming!"